Roscoe's Leap

Roscoe's Leap

Gillian Cross

with an afterword by the author

Oxford University Press
Oxford Toronto Melbourne

Oxford University Press,
Walton Street, Oxford OX2 6DP

*Oxford New York Toronto
Delhi Bombay Calcutta Madras Karachi
Petaling Jaya Singapore Hong Kong Tokyo
Nairobi Dar es Salaam Cape Town
Melbourne Auckland*

and associated companies in
Berlin Ibadan

Oxford is a trade mark of Oxford University Press

First published 1987
First published in this edition 1992

ISBN 0 19 271694 8

Printed and bound in Great Britain by
Biddles Ltd, Guildford and King's Lynn

Chapter 1

Stephen walked along the gallery with the *Daily Telegraph* under his arm, a bottle of milk in one hand and half a pound of frozen mince in the other. His trainers were almost silent, padding from diamond to daisy to diamond on the elaborate parquet floor. But no one would have heard him if he had run across in hobnailed boots. The noise of water drowned out everything else.

It was all round him. Rain hammered on the massive glass arch of the roof, bouncing off its curving ribs with their festoons of cast iron flowers. It sluiced down the huge sloping windows and spattered on their metal frames. And underneath was the stream. It crashed down the waterfall on the left—higher than the house and only fifty feet away—roared through the narrow channel under the building and tumbled steeply over rocks to the bottom of the valley.

Stephen sniffed. The smell of mould got stronger every day. There was a patch at the base of one wall and a bigger patch round the door at the far end. The broken floorboard was sagging badly too, and the windows on the waterfall side were covered with green slime. Day by day he watched the gallery rot, but he couldn't do anything about it. It was No Man's Land, not belonging to either part of the house.

When he came to the closed door at the far end of the gallery he stopped, being very careful not to touch the bellstring. He knew, from experience, that the slightest tug would set the huge brass bell ringing. And bring someone to the door.

He put down the things he was carrying. Milk, news-paper, meat, in a neat straight line on the floor. Above them on the wall was a flimsy rack cobbled together out of old bits of wood and painted a dingy pink. Stephen held his breath as he lifted the empty milk bottle out of it. One day that rack was going to fall off the wall and come crashing to the ground. But not today, thank goodness.

He pulled out the note tucked into the top of the empty milk bottle.

> *Do come in for a chat if you've got time. But—just in case I miss you—we could do with some more lavatory paper before Friday. And a couple of sixty watt light bulbs. Everything else as normal. All is well.*
> *It would be nice to see you.*
> *D.*

The usual sort of note. As usual, Stephen tucked it into his pocket and began to walk back along the gallery. Not exactly creeping, but taking care to avoid unnecessary noise.

He was halfway when the front doorbell clanged, from his own side of the house. The dull boom resounded, hanging in the air, and he slowed down to give Hannah a chance to get there before he did. Snoopers took much more notice of an almost-grownup fifteen year old girl than they did of a twelve year old boy. And it had to be a snooper. Anyone who knew them would have the sense to squeeze round, past the line of laurel bushes, and hammer at the kitchen entrance. There weren't many visitors like that anyway. But two or three times a year a snooper came across the entry in Pevsner's *Buildings of England*:

> ROSCOE'S LEAP 4m W. An idiosyncratic house by R.N. Fothergill built in 1879 for Samuel Roscoe, the millionaire sewage contractor. It has an iron framework and the main parts of the structure are of poured and shuttered concrete with dressings of York Stone. It stands immediately below the

> Falls of May, rising in irregular clusters
> of Neo-Gothic turrets on either side of
> the Mapling Beck. But its most extra-
> ordinary feature is the central section,
> which actually bridges the beck. The
> bottom floor of this is a windowless
> service corridor, above which is a forty
> foot gallery, built almost entirely of
> glass in a cast iron framework . . .

Somehow, snoopers always took that for an invitation. They struggled hopefully up the broken drive, with their maps and cameras, as if all the PRIVATE KEEP OUT notices were invisible.

The front bell boomed again. No sign of Hannah. Sisters! He was ready to bet that she was down in the furnace room again. And Mother had rattled off to town in the car, to do the month's shopping. Stephen pulled a sour face to himself as he stepped out of the gallery on to the main staircase, back into the clean, wax-polished smell of their own side of the house.

He went down the ten steps that led into the main entrance hall and hid the empty milk bottle behind the huge Japanese urn at the bottom of the stairs. Industry and Commerce and Art and Manufactures ogled him from their niches, clutching paintbrushes and bits of machinery uncomfortably in the folds of their drapery. Stephen pulled a face at Art, because she was the smuggest, and went to open the front door.

'Afraid I've had a bit of an accident . . .'

A tall, thin, young man was standing in the shadows of the huge porch, looking mournfully out from under a dripping souwester. Everything else about him seemed to be dripping as well—his nose, his glasses, his enormous mackintosh and the Ordnance Survey map tucked under one arm. In the other hand he was holding a long metal rod, entwined with ugly metal leaves.

'You've broken the bell-pull!' Stephen said, before he could stop himself.

7

The young man went pink. 'I thought no one had heard me ring. So I just gave it an extra tug and—'

Stephen glanced at the broken end. Snapped bolt. Nothing Hannah couldn't mend. A pity, really. If the thing had been really smashed up, they would have had an excuse to fit a sensible, electric bell. 'That's the original bell-pull,' he said severely. 'Put in when the house was built.'

'I know.' The young man looked even more miserable. 'Samuel Roscoe designed it himself, with all the little leaves. To show off what Hazelbury's Metal Extruder could do.'

'He did?' Stephen went very still. *That* wasn't in Pevsner.

The young man nodded and pushed his glasses back up his nose. 'He wasted thousands on that Metal Extruder. Hazelbury was the only person who ever took him for a ride. Everything else he touched turned to gold.' Suddenly he stopped lecturing and grinned. 'But I bet you know all that already, don't you?'

Stephen looked coldly polite. He was not interested in his great-great-grandfather. 'Is there something I can do for you?'

'Oh. I should have said.' The grin vanished and was replaced by an apologetic frown. 'But I thought you'd guessed. I've come to see Mr Roscoe. Mr Ernest Roscoe.'

At least that was easy to squash. 'I'm afraid my great-uncle doesn't see visitors.'

'But I'm Nick Honeyball. I'm writing a thesis.'

Stephen went on looking polite and blank.

'I've got—wait a moment—the letter's in one of my pockets.' Nick Honeyball began to burrow inside his mackintosh, showering water over Stephen. 'I'm not sure— Oh yes, here it is. Triumph!'

The moment Stephen saw the shaky, uneven copperplate writing on the envelope, he knew the letter meant trouble. Uncle Ernest was bound to have forgotten all about it. Or changed his mind. But Nick Honeyball was waving it around like a passport and it was impossible to avoid reading it.

It was even worse than he had expected.

Dear Mr Honeyball,

You will never understand Samuel Roscoe unless you come to Roscoe's Leap. He is everywhere in this house and this house is all that remains of him.

Come for as long as you like, and search out the truth. My nephew's family will be delighted to welcome you and show you round. As for me—

Eheu fugaces, Postume, Postume,
Labuntur anni

—I am an old man and can promise nothing.

O vraiment marâtre Nature!

But I hope to live to read your thesis.

Ernest Roscoe.

Stephen read it twice, playing for time. He could see that it hung together and actually made some kind of sense. To a stranger. But—*My nephew's family will be delighted to welcome you* . . . No, it was impossible.

'Extraordinary, isn't it?' Nick Honeyball was saying. 'To think of old Sam's grandson being able to quote Latin and French when Sam got all his schooling on building sites and down sewers.' He looked anxiously at Stephen. 'It *is* all right, isn't it? I mean, I've come a long way, and—'

'I think,' Stephen said, 'that you'd better come in.' He was trying to work out which way Mother would jump if she were here. The Gracious Lady or the Big Freeze? It wasn't exactly easy to turn someone away when he came with an invitation from the owner of the house. 'Shall I take your coat?'

'Mmm?' Nick Honeyball said vaguely. He was standing in the middle of the entrance hall, dripping all over the floor and gazing round with wide eyes, like a child in Disneyland.

'Your coat.'

'Oh. Yes. Of course. Sorry.' He stripped off the mac, managing to shake off every last drop of water in the process, and held it out to Stephen. Underneath he was wearing jeans and a tee-shirt which said HENRY VIII WAS A SEXIST CREEP.

Stephen swallowed and looked away. 'I think I'll go and fetch my sister. She's down in the furnace room.'

That was meant to get across the message *We're all working hard and we haven't got time to bother with you really.* But it was a total failure. Instead of looking apologetic, Nick Honeyball suddenly looked wildly excited.

'Hetherington's New Improved Vesuvius? Is it still there? Can I—may I—?'

Stephen hardly dared to think what Hannah would say if he produced a stranger to interrupt her while she was working.'It's not very beautiful down there Mr Honeyball—'

'Nick, *please*.' The eyes behind the glasses looked distressed, as if *Mister* was a deadly insult. Stephen almost shuddered. How could anyone bear to let his feelings show so clearly in his face? 'I'm not after beauty, anyway. I'm a historian and I'm interested in what happened in this house and what it's left behind. So I need to see everything. I mean—that is, if it's not too much trouble.'

He collapsed into confusion, trying to ask for what he wanted and apologize, both at the same time, and Stephen gave up arguing. It was difficult to put down someone who was busy putting himself down.

'All right Mr—all right, Nick. We go through here.'

'The door into the servants' corridor?' Nick said reverently. 'Housekeeper's room, still room, china closet, kitchen, scullery, butler's pantry, knife room . . .'

And a nasty warren of little dark cubbyholes they were too, Stephen thought as he shut the door behind them. However hard Mother scrubbed and polished, they always smelt of cabbage and old gravy. 'You don't sound as though you need a guided tour,' he said politely.

'Oh, I've seen the plans and read Samuel Roscoe's letters to Fothergill, the architect.' Nick tried to peer into the housekeeper's room as they passed. 'But to be really *here*—I can't tell you what it feels like.'

For one terrible moment, Stephen was afraid he would try, but luckily they reached the end of the corridor before he could begin.

'We go down here.' Stephen opened the door on the left, which led to the cellar steps.

Nick hesitated for a second and glanced at the other door, straight ahead. 'That leads to the servants' corridor across the beck? To the other side of the water? Could I just—?'

Stephen went very stiff. 'It's locked. We don't—we don't use that corridor.'

Nick looked faintly puzzled, but he got the message. Without asking any more questions, he went where Stephen pointed.

'Be careful on the steps,' said Stephen. 'They're very wet and slimy.'

'I know. Blasted out of solid rock.' Nick nodded and ran a hand down the damp, irregular wall as he went. 'You've got to admire the old man's stubbornness, haven't you?'

'Yes,' Stephen lied politely. He hated to think of all the money Samuel Roscoe had wasted by stubbornly insisting on building his house in that impossible place. 'We go through this cellar and into the next one.'

The second cellar was huge and dark, but someone had propped a powerful flashlight at the side of the furnace so that it loomed dramatically out of the shadows. Battleship grey and ten feet long, with thick pipes writhing out of it in all directions.

Stephen took a step towards it. 'Hannah?'

Blast Hetherington. Rot his New Improved Vesuvius Furnace. And above all, blast and rot and DAMN his Modern Scientific Heating and Ventilation System.

Hannah lay on the floor at the back of the furnace and wished she could slam her biggest wrench into the middle of the works. She'd spent the whole holiday so far tightening things and loosening things and adjusting dials and levers, but she was no nearer getting any sense out of the beastly thing than she had been in the beginning. Hetherington must have meant it to have a full-time engineer and a staff of mechanics. And in four weeks it would be the end of the summer holidays (so-called). Normally it was a relief to be back at school, where things were fairly sane and there was a gap of a hundred and forty miles between her and Roscoe's Leap. But if she couldn't fix this furnace before the end of the holidays it would have to be left until December. Which meant *another* winter of chilblains and freezing cold rooms with nasty little paraffin heaters that couldn't even melt the ice on the windows.

The whole heating system was worn out. As out of date as a dinosaur trap. It ought to be ripped out and replaced with a new gas boiler. No use trying to persuade Uncle Ernest to spend that much money, though. If you said anything to him about the house, he just went blank and switched off.

The only good thing about the past, thought Hannah savagely, *is that it's past.* She banged the nearest bit of pipe angrily with her fist and it juddered at her.

'Hannah!'

Typical Stephen! He knew she was working. He'd even agreed that it would be a good idea to try and get the heating going. But the moment she started to get down to it, he came crashing in and disturbed her. Well, he could—

She opened her mouth to yell at him, but, just in time, she looked under the pipes and saw the feet. *Two* pairs of feet. Stephen's battered old trainers and a pair of bright yellow wellingtons covered in mud.

Hannah swore silently at the pipes, pulled the rubber band off her hair and smoothed it roughly. Then she wriggled out, hoping that Mother wasn't around to see the state of her skirt.

'Mr Honeyball—Nick—this is my sister Hannah,' Stephen said, almost before she was standing up.

Hannah nodded and held out her hand. Then she saw the layer of dirt on it and put it behind her back instead. 'Hallo.' Stephen must be crazy, bringing a stranger down here. A dripping wet, nosy stranger, as well.

He knew exactly what she was thinking, of course. 'Nick's writing a thesis,' he said quickly. 'About Samuel Roscoe.'

The dripping wet stranger looked modest. 'About "Social

Mobility and the Nature of Success as exemplified in the career of Samuel Roscoe" actually.'

'Very nice,' Hannah said. He was obviously a crackpot as well as a snooper. Stephen must have had a total brainstorm to let him in at all.

'He's got a letter,' Stephen said. 'From Uncle Ernest. Saying we'd show him round the house. So I thought you and I could—'

Hannah glared at him and looked over her shoulder at the furnace. 'But I've only just started work.'

'Don't mind me. Please,' Nick said anxiously. He seemed a pretty anxious sort of person altogether. 'I'll be perfectly happy down here for a bit if you want to go on with what you're doing.'

He meant it, too. Whipped out a notebook and started peering round, scribbling every now and then. Hannah got close enough to hiss in Stephen's ear.

'Are you *out of your mind?*'

'But I couldn't just—' Stephen shrugged and looked obstinate. 'If you'd read the letter, you'd understand. Uncle Ernest's told him he can spend as much time here as he likes.'

'But what about Mother?'

Stephen shook his head. He was so *feeble*, always wanting her to sort things out as if he was thirty years younger instead of only three. Hannah snorted and looked at Nick who had got himself into the middle of the tangle of pipes. Not much use trying to do anything useful with *him* around. And she didn't like the way he was poking at the main Steam Pressure Gauge.

'O.K., O.K.,' she muttered. 'We'll do the guided tour of everything that's open. But I'm not unlocking all the spare bedrooms and things. Mother can sort that out when she comes back. *If* she doesn't have a fit. Now let's get him out of here before he blows us up.'

She raised her voice. Polite voice, for visitors. 'Mr Honeyball—' ('Nick!' Stephen hissed at her.) '—we could start in the library. Most of the papers and things are there.'

That shifted him all right. He looked up like a puppy

who's just heard someone say 'Walkies!' Hannah did the polite smile and led the way.

'It's all so wonderfully preserved,' Nick said in her ear as he came up the cellar stairs behind her. 'I never imagined that the old Vesuvius would still be around.'

'Everything possible has been left as it was,' said Hannah solemnly. 'The only alterations are the electric wiring and a couple of extra bathrooms. They were done when Uncle Ernest was a boy. Around nineteen ten.'

'Fantastic,' Nick breathed.

Hannah thought of the terrifying worn-out tangle of electric wiring with all the insulation falling off it and pulled a face to herself as she opened the door at the top of the steps. 'I suppose it is rather—unusual.'

A pity she couldn't see Stephen's face. He knew exactly what she thought of the state of the house. But his expression wasn't likely to be giving much away. His face might just as well be carved out of a block of wood.

She led the way briskly along the servants' corridor, not giving anyone a chance to stop. It was impossible to remember what all those silly little rooms were meant for. And Nick must have seen the entrance hall when he came in. So she went straight across and pushed open the library door. 'Here you are.'

It took an effort not to wrinkle her nose. The library looked towards the waterfall and there was a steep bank outside the windows. The whole place was hopelessly damp. Clean of course—Mother nearly killed herself seeing to that—but musty and cold. And even Mother couldn't *quite* keep pace with the mould.

Nick smelt it too, of course. He looked faintly unhappy as he wandered off down the room, peering into alcoves and studying the book titles.

The room was pretty misery-making anyway. Everything, but *everything* was patterned. Carved bookshelves, stained glass windows, panelled ceiling painted with flowers. *And* a huge, dark squiggly fireplace. *And* a row of hideous ornaments along the top of the bookcases. *And* complicated designs on the carpet and the curtains. *And*—

The whole thing chattered and gibbered at you like a cageful of quarrelling monkeys and it made Hannah's head ache. No rhyme or reason to it. Nothing *useful* about all that decoration. She could hardly bear to think what it must all have cost. Or how much they could have raised by selling it off.

Nick seemed to like it, though. He prowled round, making notes, turning ornaments upside down to read the marks on the bottom, fingering the books. The first time he pulled one out, he frowned and ran a finger over the leather cover. It left a dark line in the dusting of pale green mould.

Then he caught sight of the red leather boxes stacked on the last set of shelves.

'Those boxes—are they—I don't want to poke my nose in, of course, but if there are any papers—'

He sounded unbearably eager. Fancy being so keen to read someone else's old junk.

'They're mostly bills and letters,' Stephen said. 'All muddled up, I'm afraid. And I think there are some old photographs.'

'Letters? Photographs?' Nick blinked excitedly. 'Would it be very rude to ask—'

Hannah couldn't stand it any longer. 'Here.' She marched down the room, heaved a couple of boxes off the shelves and lumped them on to the big desk in the middle of the room. 'Look at them all you want. I should think they're utterly boring.'

Stephen frowned at her, of course. *Not* how she ought to be talking to a visitor. But Nick gave an unexpected grin.

'Don't worry. My family think I'm mad as well. My mother always says I was born with a notebook in one hand and a bundle of old bills in the other.'

Hannah grinned back. He looked as though he might be quite human. No reason why he shouldn't do something with those old papers, after all. It was pretty stupid having them clutter the place up if no one was ever going to look at them. She leaned over as he began to sort through the first box.

'Look—that photograph must be old. All the women

have got long dresses and hats on.'

'Edwardian.' Nick peered at it. 'Looks like a house party. It might be interesting to find out—'

But he never got to the end of the sentence. Footsteps clipped sharply across the hall and someone opened the library door. There was a tiny, startled pause. Exactly the right length. Then Mother's voice, ominously polite.

'Good afternoon. I didn't realize we had a visitor.'

Chapter 2

Stephen's skin prickled uncomfortably. Mother was smiling as she came down the room, and holding out her hand, but he knew that she was furious by a hundred tiny signs. The stiff set of her shoulders. The small, quick steps. The fixed extra-brightness of the smile.

'This is Nick Honeyball, Mother,' he said, before she had quite reached them. 'He's come—that is, Uncle Ernest's invited him to do some work on his thesis here.'

Mrs Roscoe raised her eyebrows, very slightly. 'Ah, so you've met Mr Roscoe?' It sounded like a polite question, if you didn't know how impossible that meeting was.

'No, I haven't, but I've got a letter. I—' Nick started rummaging again, dropping his pen and notebook on the floor. 'But I can't seem to find—'

'It's here.' Hannah pulled the letter out of the fallen notebook and held it up to Mrs Roscoe.

Who didn't take it.

'That's Mr Honeyball's letter, Hannah.'

'No—please—I meant you to read it—' Nick had somehow been put in the wrong, and he stumbled and stuttered and turned pink. Stephen looked down at the floor. It was too embarrassing to watch. But even then, he could see Nick's feet, with the weight shifting nervously from one to the other, backwards and forwards.

'Thank you, Mr Honeyball.' Mrs Roscoe took the letter. No accidental giveaways about her. She was small and thin and very, very straight and every word she spoke was carefully controlled.

'Please call me Nick,' Nick said, but she simply went on reading the letter as though she had not heard him. Stephen found that he was impatient to know what she would do when she had finished it. At last she looked up.

'We're very happy to have you here, Mr—er—' She glanced at the letter to check his name. Stephen had never known her to forget a name except on purpose. 'Mr Honeyball. But I must apologize for my children. Presumably they haven't yet introduced you to their great-uncle.'

'But the letter says—' Stephen began.

His mother frowned, almost imperceptibly, and he stopped. Of course. She knew quite well what the letter said. He watched her smile graciously at Nick. 'Stephen and Hannah will take you across to the other section of the house, where Mr Roscoe lives. I'm sure he will want to welcome you in person.'

No prizes for working out what she meant by *that*. If Doug had let Uncle Ernest write that letter, he ought to cope with the results. Even Hannah understood, because she looked sideways at Stephen and rolled her eyes.

But Nick seemed to miss all the undercurrents. He grinned like an idiot and pushed his glasses up his nose. 'We're going over the water? Through the gallery?'

Mrs Roscoe smiled frostily. 'I see you know about the house.'

'I've been working on the plans and the correspondence. But to have the chance of seeing it all—' Nick waved his hands helplessly in the air for a moment, as though there were no words to describe what he meant, and then gave Mrs Roscoe his disarming grin. 'Oh well, you don't need *me* to tell you what a fantastic building this is. It must be fabulous to *live* in it.'

Stephen almost shuddered, but Mrs Roscoe's answering smile was no clue to her feelings. It was just as cold and tight as the one before.

'Living here is a trust. And I've done all I can to preserve things. On *this* side of the house.' She held out her hand. 'I hope to see you later, Mr Honeyball.'

Stephen got the message, even before she glanced at him. There was shopping to unpack and a meal to cook and Stephen and Hannah wouldn't be there to help, because of

18

the visitor they had let in. She would be doing it all on her own, so the least they could do was take Nick away, so that she could get on with it.

'We'll take you to Uncle Ernest now,' he said, feeling guilty and angry, both at the same time.

'Yes. Yes of course.' Nick hurried forward and tripped over the movable library steps. Hannah rescued him before he could crash into the glass case full of stuffed humming-birds. '*Sorry.*' He went even pinker than before.

Mrs Roscoe's smile was beginning to look rather strained and Stephen hurried the others out of the door, before she could pile up any more grievances. Not that she would say, of course, but she would make certain that he and Hannah knew how she felt.

Hannah managed to steer Nick along the hall and up the stairs without letting him stop to examine anything. He seemed ridiculously over-excited and Stephen waited for him to collapse with disappointment when he actually saw the gallery.

It must have been spectacular once, when it was first built. Fine views of the waterfall and the gorge, and a forest of potted palms down the middle. But now it was just like a decaying greenhouse. Surely no one could admire that.

Nick walked slowly down the centre, staring round as if he had just got off a train and found himself in Paradise. He didn't even bother with the notebook this time. Just opened his eyes wide and grinned all over his face.

'What a way to thumb your nose at the world.'

It sounded like a joke, and Stephen gave a polite, noncommittal laugh. But Hannah frowned. She would never pretend to understand if she didn't. Not even to save trouble.

'What are you talking about?'

'Well, he was showing off wasn't he?' Nick said. 'Spitting in the eye of the local nobs, because they still thought of him as Sam Roscoe the local stonemason's son. And once Fothergill had told him he *couldn't* build a house on this site, he was set on doing it.'

'Pity he didn't fit it with windscreen wipers,' Hannah

said, staring at the green, slimy haze that almost hid the waterfall.

Stephen kicked her ankle. 'Don't you think we ought to go on?'

With a last, hungry look round, Nick nodded. 'Yes. Sorry.' He glanced towards the closed door at the far end of the gallery. 'That's where your great-uncle lives, is it? You've split the house into two?'

'Yes. More or less.' Stephen said it quickly. Just in case Hannah felt she ought to explain properly. But Hannah was looking at her watch. Probably worrying about getting back to the furnace. 'We have to ring the bell.'

Somehow the bell looked much, much worse with Nick gazing at it. As a bell it was fine. Beautiful, even, if you liked things that were elaborately engraved all over. But Doug had hung it from a plastic bracket on the wall and the weight of the metal pulled the plastic down, out of shape. The string round the clapper didn't help, either. It was green and faded and frayed with age.

Hannah put her hands behind her back, waiting for Stephen to do the ringing. And he waited for her. Each watching the other, not wanting to be the first to move. Nick looked up suddenly and saw them.

'I'll do it, shall I? I'm the visitor, after all.' There was no comment in his voice. He sounded as if he was ringing the bell for fun. He reached out for the green string and Stephen held his breath in case the string snapped, or the bracket broke and the bell came crashing to the floor.

Nick jerked the string and the clapper rattled against the bell. It gave out a cracked, sour note that died instantly, and the three of them stood waiting in the draught that came under the door. A warm draught, sickly-sweet with the smell of the air-freshener that Doug used. Stephen hated that air-freshener. Not only because it smelt foul, but because he couldn't bear to think of the other, nastier smells that it must be covering up.

Then the footsteps came across the lobby and down the stairs. He didn't take long to arrive. This side of the house was much smaller. Smoking room, billiard room, gun room, business room—the men's half of the house. And now—Stephen stopped thinking that thought and watched the doorhandle turn.

'Stephen! And Hannah!' Doug's smile was too much, as usual. He came forward with his big, pale hands outstretched, and it was all Stephen could do not to step away backwards. To disguise that, he began talking quickly.

'Uncle Ernest wrote to invite Mr Honeyball to come and work here. For his thesis.'

It came out like an accusation, but it was obvious that Doug was as surprised as they were. The eagerness died out of his face and he rubbed a puzzled hand across his balding forehead.

Nick noticed the surprise, of course. He would have had to be blind to miss it. 'I hope it's not too much trouble. Mr Roscoe did imply in his letter that his health was bad, but—'

'Mother told us to bring Nick over here,' Hannah said abruptly.

That changed things, of course. Immediately, Doug was smiling as hard as he could. He turned to Nick and held out his hand. 'And you're Mr Honeyball?'

'Oh, sorry.' Stephen had been too rattled to remember the introductions. 'This is Nick Honeyball. Nick, this is—' He hesitated, and before he could make up his mind what to say Doug finished the sentence for him.

'I'm Doug. Please come in.'

Same old Doug, thought Hannah. The *fuss*! Anyone would think he hadn't seen them for five years, when it was only—what? Three weeks? Two? She and Stephen had trotted across to pay their ritual visit when they got back from school, all washed and scrubbed and dressed in their best. And she'd been over by herself once, as well, because Doug had had some sort of trouble with the toaster and lost half the screws when he took it to bits. If they were over there every couple of days, they'd never have time to *do* anything.

Angrily making excuses to herself, she followed Stephen

and Nick through the door and looked round to see what Doug had been up to since she was last there. Oh yes. A couple of typical Dougish improvements. Last time the wallpaper had been peeling off the wall opposite, hanging down in great loops. Now it had been stuck back up with Sellotape, not quite straight. And there was a rail fixed round the wall, at elbow level. For Uncle Ernest to hang on to? Hannah touched it gingerly and hoped not. A couple of tugs and those screws would pull straight out of the plaster.

Nick was clutching his notebook and staring round as if he was too paralysed to write anything. At the screw-holes and the Sellotape and the orange plastic lampshade hanging six feet above their heads.

'Difficult to adapt an old place like this for an invalid,' Doug said, 'but I do what I can to make it comfortable.' He stopped outside the door of Uncle Ernest's little sitting room. 'We're just about to have coffee. You're welcome to join us, but I'd better go in first. To prepare him. If he's taken by surprise, he might be rather—'

He ducked inside and closed the door, without finishing the sentence. Yes, Hannah thought grimly, Uncle Ernest probably would be rather. He always was rather, as far as she could see.

'I thought—' Nick looked unhappy. 'I thought you said that nothing had been touched.'

'On *our* side of the house,' Stephen said. 'Over here— well, there have been a few adaptations.'

Adaptations! Hannah felt like squawking with laughter. More like wholesale alterations. Doug was the sort of do-it-yourselfer who couldn't see something without wanting to turn it into something else. Homemade polythene double glazing on all the sash windows. Electric bells in every room, that would have given you quite a shock if you'd tried to use them. Fireplaces ripped out so that the chimney breasts could be turned into cupboards. Only the cupboard doors never closed and the cupboards were full of soot.

Nick glanced up at the orange lampshade again and closed his eyes. 'And the smoking room?' he said faintly.

Hannah remembered. Sort of. 'That's what Uncle

Ernest's sitting room used to be, isn't it?'

'The smoking room may be thought excessive,' Nick said, without opening his eyes. He was talking in the kind of voice people use when they're quoting. 'But the Moorish setting, so suitable to the consumption of tobacco, may not be achieved without a richness and attention to detail that only the finest craftsmen can attain. For myself, I find it pleasant and relaxing, if somewhat dark.'

Hannah had a quick mental picture of the coating of white paint daubed all over the walls of the sitting room and its complicated, carved ceiling. 'I think it may have been rather *too* dark for a sitting room,' she said carefully. 'But it's still got lots of little alcoves and things.'

'It has?' Stephen said.

'Of course it has.' Hannah felt like shaking him. He was so unobservant. 'Of course it has. All those little spaces with twiddly arches, where Doug's put shelves up. And the television cupboard.'

Nick looked even more miserable.

'Ah, here comes Doug,' Hannah said brightly.

It was quite funny, really. Poor old Nick braced himself, as if he was about to see something frightful. Straightened his shoulders and lifted his chin. Then he stepped through the door and immediately forgot all about the decorations of the room, because he was too busy trying not to stare at Uncle Ernest.

Which was pretty difficult. How do you ignore a man-mountain in grey dressing-gown encrusted with old bits of food? He was six foot tall and four foot wide and he overflowed his wheelchair in all directions. But he obviously wasn't in a very bright mood. His head was slumped forward on to his chest and he was gazing at a hole in the toe of his slipper.

'He's not likely to say much,' Doug hissed in Hannah's ear. 'He's having a bad day. Very low.'

Oh great. Why not say that before? Now it was too late to warn Nick, because he had already started in on his pretty speech.

'. . . very kind of you to invite me here . . . invaluable

opportunity . . . remarkable house . . .'

The huge, slumped head didn't move an inch. There was no sign at all that Nick was getting through and gradually his voice faltered and stopped. Then he glanced over his shoulder at Doug and mouthed '*Is he deaf?*'

Hannah almost snorted. She could never make up her mind about Uncle Ernest. Was he too switched off to notice what anyone was doing, or did he get some kind of twisted, senile pleasure out of listening to people trying to talk to him? Whichever it was, he certainly wasn't deaf. When it suited him, he could hear a whisper on the other side of a closed door.

But Doug did not pay any attention to Nick's question. He was too busy pushing up chairs and dragging a small table to one side of the wheelchair. An octagonal table that had once been elegant. Now it had a sort of plastic railing fixed round five of its eight sides, to stop Uncle Ernest knocking his cup off it, and great screw-holes broke the smooth, rosewood surface. Hannah couldn't *imagine* fixing a few simple screws as badly as that.

'Coffee time already, Ernest,' Doug said brightly. 'And I've got chocolate biscuits. Your favourite. I must have guessed we were having visitors. Are you feeling hungry?'

That endless chatter, spattered with bright questions that didn't expect an answer. Perhaps it wasn't surprising that Uncle Ernest switched off. Hannah felt like putting her fingers in her ears. Instead, she sat down and took a biscuit. Chewing it slowly, she thought about Hetherington's New Improved Vesuvius. No point in wasting time.

Doug hovered for a moment, looking anxiously from Uncle Ernest to the full coffee cup on the little table. Then he glanced at Stephen. 'I'll just go and make some more coffee. Could you—?' A wink and a nod. As if they wouldn't have known anyway!

Doug hurried out and left the three of them staring at Uncle Ernest. Not exactly Host of the Year, Hannah thought sourly. For two or three minutes he didn't move at all, and she wondered, half-horrified and half-fascinated, whether they would know if he had died.

Dear Ernest, you're looking a little pale today. Hardly with us at all, are you? And your hands are distinctly chilly . . .

Suddenly, one of the big hands moved.

It fumbled its way up to the table to find the handle of the coffee cup, and there was a tenser silence. All three of them held their breath, waiting for the cup to go over. It would have been funny if it wasn't so creepy. Stephen was sitting on the edge of his chair and Nick's hand had stopped halfway to his mouth, holding his chocolate biscuit in midair, as he watched for the sudden jerk that would send coffee flooding everywhere.

But Uncle Ernest's hand didn't jerk. It lifted the coffee cup and carried it slowly across the gap between the table and the wheelchair. Then the enormous mouth opened, showing scattered yellow teeth, and Uncle Ernest drank a few mouthfuls of coffee.

Back went the cup. Stephen was almost falling off his chair now and Nick's fingers were smeared with melted chocolate. Uncle Ernest fumbled round the side of his saucer, found the plate of biscuits and took one. He still hadn't looked at any of them, but Hannah was sure he knew just what was going on. *I bet you're killing yourself laughing at us, you horrible old man.*

She tapped her foot against Stephen's ankle. 'Say something.' It was all his fault, after all. He was the one who had let Nick in in the first place, and now poor Nick was so embarrassed that he could hardly breathe. Someone ought to try and make things seem a bit more normal.

Stephen had a fair try. 'Nick—er—Mr Honeyball's thesis sounds really interesting, Uncle Ernest. It's about—um—social mobility and success—um—especially Samuel Roscoe's. He—'

Uncle Ernest reached for his coffee cup again and Stephen stuttered and stopped. Hannah decided to help him out.

'Mr Honeyball knows an awful lot about Samuel Roscoe. Isn't that right, Stephen?'

'Oh yes. Much more than we do.' Stephen glanced at Nick. 'You said you've been reading his letters. Did they give you any idea of what sort of person he was?'

Suddenly Uncle Ernest's massive head lifted, as though the question had penetrated his brain. He looked round slowly and fixed his eyes not on Stephen but on Nick, waiting for him to speak.

'I can hardly—' Nick blushed. 'I mean, it's ridiculous for *me* to be telling *you* what Samuel Roscoe was like.' He looked back at Uncle Ernest. 'You must have known him. That's the sort of question I wanted to ask you.'

Uncle Ernest didn't reply, of course. He just went on staring at Nick, with the same fixed stare, hardly blinking. Waiting for Nick to say what he thought about Samuel Roscoe. For a couple of seconds more, Nick shuffled with embarrassment, but then he gave in. And the moment he started to talk, he was like a different person. Enthusiastic. Almost glowing. It took Hannah's breath away.

'He was—well, he was a fantastic man. To start with nothing like that, with a father who drank and a mother who had twelve children and who was always ill—that takes incredible willpower. He was on his own from when he was fourteen, you know, and he made his own way by sheer hard work. Digging all day and studying all night, seven days a week, for years and years and years.'

'Studying?' Hannah said. She thought of the tall, stern man in the portrait on the drawingroom wall. He didn't look as though he'd ever been anything as humble as a learner. But Nick was nodding eagerly.

'Taught himself. He probably knew more about sewers than anyone else in Europe, and he was a millionaire by the time he was fifty. He—'

Before he could go on, a voice interrupted him. A deep voice but thin, with no substance to it. The ghost of a rumbling bass.

'Drains,' said Uncle Ernest. 'That's what this house was built on. Drains.'

It was so unexpected, so *ridiculous*, that Hannah gave a quick choke of laughter before she could stop herself. Nick shook his head at her, smiling.

'Nothing funny about drains. Imagine life without them.'

I know more about drains than you do, Hannah wanted to say. *I bet you've never unblocked a drain in your life.* But that would have been rude.

'I don't think Samuel Roscoe thought *anything* was funny,' she muttered. 'There's a picture of him in the drawing room, and he doesn't look as if he ever laughed at all.'

Uncle Ernest's head turned towards her so sharply that she nearly dropped her chocolate biscuit when she met his stare. Horrible eyes he had, too. Dark and bloodshot, with the whites all going yellow.

'He laughed,' he said fiercely. 'He *laughed*.'

It was creepy, because it meant something. She could feel the meaning, heavy in the words, trying to get across to her, but it was failing. *So what? So he did laugh. What's earth-shaking about that?* Uncle Ernest looked round pettishly, like a sulky child.

'Doug? Where is he? *Doug!*'

'Here I am, here I am.' Doug pushed the door open with one hand, balancing a tray of coffee cups in the other. 'Trusty old Doug is on his way with coffee for everyone and—'

Uncle Ernest banged a fist on the arm of his wheelchair. 'Shut up!'

Hannah wished Doug had looked insulted, or even surprised at being spoken to like that. She didn't want to know that he was used to it. But he just put down the tray on top of a bookcase and walked over to Uncle Ernest, laying a hand gently on his shoulder.

'All right. What is it?'

'I want you—'

The words disappeared for a moment and they all watched as Uncle Ernest mouthed, fumbling for them with his lips. Then he got a grip on what he wanted to say and his head went up triumphantly.

'Take them to see the Collection.'

Chapter 3

Take them to see the Collection.

In Stephen's memory, something huge and dark moved suddenly out of the shadows. A pain along the side of his head and voices shouting and someone—himself?— screaming and screaming and screaming . . .

His hand jerked, snapping his biscuit in two.

'Collection?' Hannah said. 'What collection?'

Vaguely, Stephen could hear Nick's voice, quick and enthusiastic, as if he had been delightfully surprised.

'Samuel Roscoe's collection of automatons? It's here? I thought it got auctioned off at Sotheby's before the First World War when he died and—'

'Not the best ones,' Doug said. For some reason his voice sounded strained. 'They're downstairs.'

'*What* collection?' Hannah said again, insistently. 'Do you mean there's a collection of mechanical toys downstairs that we don't even know about?'

'You were at school,' Doug said vaguely. 'Away. But Stephen—'

Chatter, chatter, chatter. A jangle of voices, irritating, like the buzzing of flies. Only one way to stop them. Stephen stood up.

'Shall we go then? If we're going.'

Biscuit crumbs scattered from his trousers and he brushed them quickly on to the carpet before anyone could see. A ridiculous, clumsy thing to have done, for absolutely no reason at all. He couldn't possibly remember anything about the collection they were going to see. He'd gone away to school himself when he was seven. Before that, most things were a blank, lost in the time when he was too young to remember anything.

'Let's go,' he said again, and this time everyone moved towards the door. Except Uncle Ernest. He sat in his wheelchair, completely still, watching them all leave. Even when the door closed behind them, Stephen could still feel the ugly, expressionless eyes following, as though they could see along corridors, round corners, down stairs.

'Excitement!' hissed Hannah sarcastically in his ear. 'Unknown territory! Or have you been this way before?'

Automatically Stephen shook his head. But immediately he knew that he was wrong. *This way*, said his mind. He could have sworn that he had never been past Uncle Ernest's sitting room, never penetrated the unused corridors on this side of the house or gone down the small staircase that led to the ground floor. But now, as he followed the others, his memory kept pace with his feet. It didn't give him any warning of what he was going to see, but as he turned each corner he recognized the view, eerily.

None of Doug's 'improvements' here. Even the dust looked as if it had not been disturbed for years. It lodged in the crevices of the carved dolphins which arched their backs on the banisters and it covered the pattern of the stair carpet with a soft grey silt.

They came down the stairs into a lobby—*yes, that's right*—decorated with paintings of dead pheasants and stags shot full of arrows. As they passed the gun room, Nick peered round the half-open door, but Stephen did not need to copy him. He could already see, in his mind, the long dull barrels of the guns and their polished stocks, inlaid with mother-of-pearl.

'Here we are,' said Doug, pushing open the next door. 'It was built as a business room, of course, but the Collection's always been stored here.'

He stepped inside and flicked on the lights. It was a narrow room, about twelve feet long. Windows ran across the short wall opposite them, but Doug did not bother to pull the heavy velvet curtains that covered them, shutting out the daylight. The electric light was dull and lifeless, and somehow brighter than Stephen remembered. He had expected flickering shadows and small, isolated pools of brightness. *You see?* he thought triumphantly, *I really don't remember*. And then wondered, with a shock, whom he was trying to convince.

The room was lined with cabinets covered by velvet cloths. Three against the left hand wall and two against the right, with a closed door in between them. Apart from the cabinets, the only furniture in the room was a long mahogany table that ran down the centre. Its dark surface reflected the frieze of medieval figures round the walls. Hooded, monkish shapes with solemn dark eyes.

Nick walked slowly down the room and touched the cloth on top of the first cabinet. 'The automatons are in here?'

Doug nodded. 'Go on. Take the cloth off.'

Soldiers, said Stephen's memory as Nick twitched at the velvet. But this time it was wrong. The cabinet was full of small animals. Some were made of painted tin, some were covered with balding fur, and a few were much richer, golden and jewelled. He noticed a squirrel holding a nut, a frog with enamelled eyes, a comic donkey.

Hannah peered through the glass. 'Do they work?'

'Some of them.' Doug opened the front of the cabinet. 'Want to see?'

He lifted out an elephant, knocking its key to the floor with a clatter. Retrieving it, he slid the key into a hole behind the elephant's ear. Suddenly he looked cheerful, for the first time since they had left Uncle Ernest.

'When I was in practice, you know, I could wind fast enough to get everything in the cabinet going at once. All those that *do* go. Shall I see if I can still do it?'

Stephen, Hannah and Nick all nodded politely and there was a metallic grinding as Doug turned the key. When he put the elephant down on the table it raised its trunk and turned its head jerkily from side to side, flapping its ears. A ridiculous piece of painted tin, no bigger than Stephen's clenched fist, with a simple clockwork mechanism. And yet—as Doug reached into the cabinet for the squirrel the elephant was like an actor alone on a vast empty stage, holding everybody's attention.

Then the squirrel joined it, nibbling the nut. The donkey, flinging its head back as it brayed. A monkey in satin clothes who played a tiny fiddle and an elegant golden lion that held out its paw to a tiny silver mouse. Doug left perhaps half a dozen of the automatons in the cabinet, but all the others joined the collection of creatures on the table, jerking, flapping, squeaking.

Each animal had a different rhythm. Every squeak or squeal was at a slightly different pitch. Stephen wanted to close his eyes and put his hands over his ears, but he went on smiling a bland, meaningless smile as Doug moved to the next cabinet, which was full of jewelled, feathered birds.

The soldiers were in the third one. Small, upright figures in outdated uniforms. Pillboxes or shakos or busbies on their head. Faded red coats, spurs like thorns and swords like darning needles. They strutted in circles and banged drums and nodded their minute metal heads. Round and round, up and down with a mindless, pointless busyness.

Before he pulled the cloth off the fourth cabinet, Doug glanced at Stephen. 'This one was your favourite. When you came before.'

Stephen stood very still, hardly breathing. But whatever he had been expecting, it was not the large, highly-coloured Noah's Ark that filled the whole cabinet. A procession of little animals stood on the gangplank, two by two and Mr and Mrs Noah waited on board, welcoming them with open arms. Doug smiled as he started to wind it up.

'You wanted to take the animals out and play with them. Remember?'

I don't remember anything.

Stephen shook his head and saw the smile wilt and Doug's eyes darken with disappointment. But it wasn't his fault, he thought angrily, watching the endless stream of animals begin to walk up the gangplank to the ark. They were set on a wheel so that they went in at the open door and round and down, to reappear through the hole in the bank, ready to do the same thing all over again. Round and round and round. And the words repeated themselves in Stephen's head like an accompanying chorus. *It's not my fault, it's not my fault, it's not my fault . . .*

Nick did not seem to be very interested in the Noah's Ark. He wandered past the closed door, to the last cabinet, and raised the corner of the cloth so that he could look at what was inside. For a second he stood, bending over so that he could peer at the shapes arranged on the shelves. Human figures, ready to sweep or dance or do acrobatics at the turn of a key. But whatever he wanted obviously was not there because he dropped the cloth and shook his head slightly, disappointed.

'Don't you want to look at those?' Doug said.

'Oh yes. Yes of course,' said Nick hastily. 'If you've got time, that is. But I was just wondering—you said some of the automatons were sold?'

'That's right. Nothing really valuable though.'

Nick frowned. 'So where's—I mean, it's none of my business, I know, but he does refer to it in his letters and I was curious—'

'Spit it out,' Hannah said, interrupting. Rudely, Stephen thought. 'What do you *want?*'

Nick grinned at her, as though he liked being insulted. Then he looked back at Doug and asked his question directly.

'What happened to the French Terror?'

Hannah had to squash down a giggle. Poor old Nick finally managed to ask a straight question and everyone was too speechless to answer. Stephen had gone dead white and Doug's mouth dropped open. She filled the gap herself, to save embarrassment.

'What's the French Terror when it's at home?'

Nick rubbed the end of his nose. 'I'm not exactly sure. Must have been something pretty special, because old Sam raved on about it in his letters. Paid a few thousand pounds for it and reckoned he'd got a bargain.'

'*Must* have been special.' Hannah whistled. 'Sounds bloodthirsty.'

'Oh, I think it had something to do with the French Revolution. Guillotines and head-choppings and bags of gore, you know.' Nick gave her that rather shy smile again. 'But I suppose it must have been sold off.'

He was too polite to ask the question again, seeing it had met with such a ravingly enthusiastic welcome. But Hannah thought he ought to get his answer. Besides, she wanted to know herself. The French Terror sounded a bit more exciting than most of these other bits of clockwork. She tapped Doug on the shoulder.

'Go on, then. What did happen to it? *Was* it sold?'

Doug's eyes flickered for a second as he glanced past her. Towards the closed door? She wasn't quite certain, but she could tell he was faking, because he was so bad at it. He gave a silly little laugh.

'Oh, *that*. I wasn't sure what you were talking about for a moment. Yes, it never really worked properly.'

Hannah just had time to register that he hadn't really answered her question, but before she could challenge him, there was a loud crash from upstairs, followed by a series of thuds as if someone was rapping on the floor.

'Ernest!' Doug looked up anxiously and Hannah wondered whether he expected Uncle Ernest to appear through the ceiling. 'I ought to go and—' He glanced helplessly at the table, which was covered with automatons, some of them still and some of them slowly running down.

'Don't worry about those,' Nick said. 'We can put those back for you. You go and see what's happened upstairs.'

Doug hesitated for an instant, but there was another volley of thumps from upstairs and he nodded. 'I think I'd better. But you will be careful—?'

Fret, fret, fret. As if she wasn't a million times better with her hands than he was. Hannah felt like pushing him out of the door. Not that she thought there was a major emergency. She was willing to bet that Uncle Ernest just wanted a bit of attention.

'We'll be all right,' she said solemnly. 'You go.'

Then, mercifully, he did and it was all she could do not to heave a sigh of relief. Ditherers drove her wild. Turning back to the table, she picked up the elephant and the squirrel and put them back in their places. Then the donkey.

There was no need to think. She had always had a good memory for where things went, ever since she took her first clock to pieces when she was a little girl. In a couple of minutes she had put away all the automatons except those that were still moving. While she was waiting for them to stop, she glanced up and her eyes fell on the closed door between the two cabinets opposite her. With a sort of idle curiosity, she remembered Doug's eyes flickering in that direction.

'I wonder what's through there,' she said. More for something to say than because she really expected an answer.

Stephen looked blank, but Nick screwed up his face comically, like someone trying to get a picture clear in his mind.

'I think—yes, it must be the billiard room. I don't remember anything else on the plans of this floor.' He looked suddenly eager. 'It's got a painted ceiling. I wouldn't mind a peep if you think it's O.K.'

'We ought not to poke about,' Stephen said quickly.

Hannah snorted. 'It's not going to do anyone any harm if we just open the door and look in, is it?' She marched across the room and grabbed the door handle. 'We needn't even—'

It was locked.

Stephen looked relieved and faintly smug, and Hannah was furious. She felt like kicking the door.

'Well,' she said sourly, 'I don't suppose it's any great loss. I expect the ceiling's fallen down and that's why the door's locked. It would be typical of the way this house is run to let a painted ceiling fall down.'

That should annoy Stephen. Complaining about the family in front of a visitor. He was such a little prig about things like that. Hannah looked apologetically at Nick.

'Does it upset you, seeing the place dropping to pieces?'

It was only a casual question really, no big deal, but the effect on Nick was startling. He went bright red in the face, struggled for a moment and then exploded into words.

'I—well, it's none of my business, of course, but I think it's wicked. *Wicked!* This beautiful house—and it's not just beautiful, it's *important*. It's what Samuel Roscoe left behind him, as a memorial. And it's just rotting, because nobody can be bothered to look after it. I think it ought to be a crime to destroy things by neglecting them! I—'

Then he suddenly heard himself. Stuttered and choked to a stop. For a moment Hannah was too amazed to say anything. He was near to tears, she could see, and all for nothing. All for a dead drain-builder's house. Studying history must have a very peculiar effect on people.

'Keeping up a house like this costs money,' she said at last, defensively.

'But Samuel Roscoe was a *millionaire*, for heaven's sake! Where has all that—' Nick swallowed and looked confused. 'I'm sorry. I didn't mean to snoop. And anyway, a house like this can earn enough to maintain itself. If anyone cares enough to take the trouble. Why don't you open it to the public?'

Hannah looked at Stephen. *Here we go again.* They'd had this argument with Mother a hundred times and both of them could recite the answer automatically.

If Uncle Ernest doesn't want the house opened, that's none of our business. He's been very good to us as it is, and we'll just have to manage as best we can.

Which, being interpreted, meant that he was paying their school fees, so Don't Rock the Boat. If he was a tight-fisted old miser who was happy to see his house drop to bits, they had to let him get on with it. Otherwise he might turn nasty and there would be no more school. No blessed escape from Roscoe's Leap and the never-ending work and—the other things that were worse than work.

Only they could hardly explain all that to a stranger. Even one as nice as Nick.

'Uncle Ernest couldn't cope with people all over the house,' Stephen said at last. 'He's too frail.'

Frail? Uncle Ernest? He was about as frail as half a ton of granite.

But Nick persisted, frowning and running a hand through his hair. 'But you don't *have* to have people running all over the house. How about letting them in just to see the automatons? They're good enough on their own. And the people could come up the back drive and in at the door on this side. They wouldn't disturb anyone.'

'The back drive's overgrown,' Stephen said obstinately.

'Well, clear it, then.' Nick waved a hand.

Hannah looked at him for a second, calculating. There was no reason why it shouldn't work. Other people opened exhibitions, and there were lots of tourists in the dale in the summer. Desperate for places to visit when it rained. Especially for children.

Nick had already noticed that she was wavering. 'Imagine being able to get the gallery windows cleaned up professionally,' he said. 'And the damp in the library dealt with. You can't do things like that by yourself, Hannah, you need people who understand the technical side. And they cost money. Imagine—'

But she didn't need him to paint her a picture. She could have sat down that instant and made a long, long list of things that needed doing to the house. That needed doing properly. The idea was magic.

'What do you think?' she said, whirling round to look at Stephen. 'We could almost take care of it on our own if we only opened in the holidays.'

Instant cold water. He gave her a pale, pinched look and shook his head. 'Mother wouldn't even let us ask.'

He was right about that. But Hannah wasn't going to give up so easily.

'What's it got to do with Mother? It would all happen on this side of the house. Why shouldn't we ask Uncle Ernest directly, without her knowing?'

Stephen hesitated and then shook his head. 'The automatons are valuable, Hannah. Uncle Ernest isn't going to let us play around with them.'

'If they're valuable, they ought to be properly looked

after,' Hannah said firmly. 'They ought to be cleaned and half of them need mending, and that's one thing I *can* do. You know I can.'

'But Uncle Ernest doesn't know.'

'He will if you tell him.' Hannah banged her hand triumphantly against the locked door. 'I can't say it, because it'll look like boasting, but you can. You'll have to be the one who goes to ask.'

He hesitated for longer this time, and Hannah looked at Nick for support. 'Go on, tell him. We've *got* to do it, haven't we?'

'It can't do any harm to ask, can it?' Nick said.

Stephen was still hesitating, but Hannah could see him getting ready to shake his head, so she gave him another prod.

'Afraid?'

'Of course not!'

It was a touchy answer, very quick, very spiky, and when she heard it she knew that she would be able to persuade him. Given a bit of time.

Chapter 4

Stephen stood just inside the drawing room, peering round the door and thinking that he must be mad. Hannah had been nagging him for a week and that must have turned his brain, otherwise he would never have been creeping round in this ridiculous way.

'Well?' hissed Hannah in his ear. 'What's going on?'

He shook his head. 'It's not five to eight yet.'

The hands on the big marble clock in the entrance hall were crawling round. Another two minutes to go before the regular Tuesday morning rubbish ritual. One minute. Thirty seconds. *Now.*

The door from the service corridor opened and Mother looked through it, peering up the hall towards the gallery. Once she was satisfied there was nobody coming, she staggered out, carrying a bulging rubbish sack in each hand. Very carefully, she placed the two sacks in the middle of the marble floor, leaning against each other. Then she disappeared back through the door, closing it after her.

Stephen watched the hands of the clock crawl round again, towards eight o'clock. Hannah poked him in the ribs.

'Is he coming?'

'It's only two minutes to,' Stephen whispered.

'He'll be early. He's always early.'

He was. At one and a half minutes to eight, Doug came down the steps from the gallery carrying another rubbish sack. Early enough to catch Mother if she hadn't been careful not to be late. He walked down the entrance hall to the rubbish sacks she had left and paused there for a moment, looking towards the closed service door. Then he picked up all the sacks, two in one hand and one in the other, and went out through the front door.

Stephen started to go out of the drawing-room, but Hannah grabbed him by the scruff of his neck and dragged him back.

'Wait!'

Of course. He'd forgotten Mother. Pulling the door almost shut again, he watched through the crack.

Ten seconds or so after the front door had closed, when Doug was safely on his way down the front drive, she came out again, with a cloth in her hand. Kneeling down, she wiped briskly over the marble slabs where the rubbish sacks had stood, and then disappeared back into the kitchen, leaving a lingering smell of disinfectant.

'Now.' Hannah gave Stephen a push that sent him halfway to the stairs and, before he had time to think again, he was crossing the gallery towards Uncle Ernest's door.

It stood ajar, the way Doug always left it when he went out. For a second Stephen hesitated on the threshold, and then he slipped through it and tiptoed up the stairs to the door of Uncle Ernest's sitting room. No sound. Cautiously he tapped on the wooden panel at the top.

Was that a grunt or a voice calling 'Come in'? Either way, it was some kind of answer. He pushed the door open and stepped inside. The wheelchair had been moved over to the fireplace and Uncle Ernest sat still and hunched, staring at the glowing coal. Stephen found it hard to breathe in the hot, close air, but Uncle Ernest's sagging cheeks were tinged blue, and his huge hands were icy-pale.

'Good morning, Uncle Ernest.'

No reply, of course. There was no way of telling whether Uncle Ernest even knew he was there. But he had to speak. The question had to be asked. Pushing his hands into his pockets, Stephen walked round to stand between the wheelchair and the fire, smiling a broad, mechanical smile. No point in dressing up what he had to say, if Uncle Ernest wasn't listening. He might as well come straight out with it.

'I've come to thank you for letting us see the Collection last week. We really enjoyed it and we had—well, we had an idea that we thought you might be interested in.'

He swallowed, feeling his smile begin to choke him. It was hard to talk to someone who was staring at the ground. But it had to be done. He took a deep breath and almost gabbled the rest.

'If we cleared the back drive, we could open the Collection to the public in the summer and make some money to repair the house.'

Nothing. And the fire was starting to feel uncomfortably hot on the backs of his legs. There was no need to say anything else, but sheer nervousness made him go on.

'Hannah could clean the automatons. And mend the ones that don't work. She's very good at things like that.'

Now he'd said everything, and he could smell the cloth of his trousers growing hot. Soon he would have to move. In his head, slowly, he began to count to twenty. *Then I'll go. One, two, three* . . .

But, as he reached sixteen, Uncle Ernest suddenly lifted his head. His eyes scanned Stephen's face for a moment or two and then he spoke.

'Alison's son.'

Stephen nodded. 'Yes.'

'And Hannah?'

'She's my sister.'

Uncle Ernest waved one hand impatiently, to show that he knew that already. 'Hannah mends?'

'Oh yes. Yes. She's always fixing things. The big clock in the entrance hall, the clockwork spit in the kitchen, with all those gears—oh, loads of things. She—'

'Yes, *yes*.' The big head turned from side to side, as if Uncle Ernest was shaking off an irritating buzzing. 'Doug tells me. All the time. But he hasn't told me this. About the Collection.'

'We haven't told him anything about it. We thought—'

Uncle Ernest lifted his head and smiled suddenly, his face gapping in the middle, grotesque as a Punch and Judy puppet. Then his hands reached down for the driving wheels of his wheelchair and he spun himself round and across the room towards the bureau in the far corner, jerking his head to show that he wanted Stephen to follow.

As Stephen approached, the big, bony hands were rummaging in the bureau drawers, finding a little brass key and fumbling to fit it into the keyhole of the desk top. But they were too clumsy. Impatiently Uncle Ernest pushed the little key at Stephen, tapping his fingers on the arm of the wheelchair while Stephen opened the desk.

'Turn your back. Shut your eyes.'

Obediently, Stephen closed his eyes and turned. There was a click. The sound of a drawer sliding open and then sliding shut again.

'Here,' said Uncle Ernest.

He was holding out a key. Not the little brass key of the bureau, but an iron one, about three inches long. He waved it about until Stephen took it from him and then he leaned back in his wheelchair and closed his eyes. But not to sleep. He began to speak in a brisk, steady voice, as though the words had been waiting in the darkness inside his head.

'You may clear the back drive and mend the automatons —but you must mend them all. Every one. And you mustn't let Doug or Alison know what you're doing.' He chuckled, out of the darkness. 'Especially not Alison.'

'But—' Stephen began.

Uncle Ernest went on talking, still with his eyes closed. 'She'll never forgive herself. First she wouldn't give up the weight, and then she jumped backwards instead of forwards. She'll be guilty for ever. Backwards . . .'

Stephen felt a shudder run up his back, between his shoulder-blades. 'But how can we get into the Collection without telling Doug? And what's this key for?'

'Backwards instead of forwards, backwards . . .'

The brisk voice had changed to a croon, and Uncle Ernest was rocking slowly in his chair, gripping the arms fiercely. The shudder spread from Stephen's back all over his skin. He couldn't bear it. The blank, closed eyes, the meaningless mumble, the repetitive movement made him want to grab the handles of the wheelchair and push it hard, towards the fire. He had to get out of the room.

'I must go now,' he said quickly. 'Thank you for the key.'

The eyelids flicked open. The yellow eyes stared at him

sharply. Uncle Ernest threw three words at him, emphasizing each one with a heavy thump of his fist.

'She—is—guilty.'

Stephen ran to the door, pulled it open, almost threw himself through it. Uncle Ernest was mad. A mad old man talking gibberish as he peered into the fire. No point in taking any notice of anything he said.

Guilty. She is guilty. She jumped backwards instead of forwards . . .

Gibberish.

He closed the door and leaned back against it, catching his breath, composing his face, getting a grip on himself. It took only thirty seconds or so, but that was too long. As he began to walk towards the stairs, he heard Doug coming in from the gallery.

Automatically, Stephen slid the long iron key into his trouser pocket, pushing it well down.

'Stephen!' Doug took the last few stairs at a run. 'Were you looking for me?'

'No, I—'

'It's a long time since we had a proper chat. Come into the kitchen and I'll make you a cup of coffee.'

'But Uncle Ernest—'

'Ernest can wait. I want to know how you've been getting on at school this term.'

Slipping an arm round Stephen's shoulders, Doug began to lead him towards the kitchen.

It would have been sensible to let it happen, just to get it over for another six months or so. All those polite questions that were painful just because they *were* polite, stranger's questions. *Are you enjoying school? How's the cricket coming along?* And then, more awkwardly, *How's your mother these days?* It was uncomfortable, but it never happened more than two or three times a year. A chat with Doug now would give him immunity at least until after Christmas.

Only he had the key, heavy and awkward in his pocket. And his head was resounding with words that were just as heavy and awkward. *You mustn't let Doug know . . .She'll be guilty for ever . . .*

'No, I've got to go. Really. I only came to—to bring something across to Uncle Ernest.'

'You could stay and have some coffee anyway.' But Doug said it without enthusiasm, as if he already knew the answer, and his arm slid back to his side.

Then, from the other side of the house, came the clang of the big front door bell, newly mended by Hannah. Stephen looked apologetic, avoiding Doug's eyes.

'I really must go and answer it.'

He began to push past, towards the stairs. As he passed, Doug said suddenly and fiercely, 'Do you *remember* that it wasn't always like this?'

At the same instant, passing so close, Stephen caught a whisper of the smell that belonged distinctively to Doug. A mixture of sweet toothpaste, aftershave and very faint, new sweat. The smell and the question, together, brought back— not a memory that he could fix on, but the feel of a memory. No picture, but an exact, precise sensation of warmth and safety, mixed inextricably with that Doug-smell.

And still the question hung in the air, waiting for an answer. Stephen swallowed.

'No,' he lied, 'I don't remember. Sorry.'

No problem about getting away now. Doug stepped back, effacing himself against the wall, and the faint almost-memory dissolved, leaving Stephen feeling relieved but oddly empty.

As he walked back across the gallery, he trod carefully on the diamonds, avoiding the daisies, trying to blot out everything except the concentration he needed to put his feet on the right pieces of polished wood.

When Hannah opened the front door to Nick, she wasn't exactly overjoyed to see him. There he was, with his tatty plastic bag full of papers, still apologizing after a week of coming to work in the library.

'I hope I haven't disturbed you. Only there's still quite a lot of work to do on those papers—'

Shut up and get on with it, then, she wanted to say, *instead of wasting my time by apologizing.* But she couldn't, of course. That would be Rude to Visitors. So she smiled and said not at all and made polite conversation for a moment or two while she wished he would go away.

And then she changed her mind, all at once.

Stephen came walking through the gallery and down the stairs, as calmly as usual, as if he hadn't just been to see Uncle Ernest. *The answer's no,* Hannah thought. She grabbed his arm as soon as he was near enough, pulled him and Nick into the drawing-room and shut the door.

'Well? What happened? What did Uncle Ernest say?'

And Nick stopped looking apologetic and sharpened up. 'You've been to ask about opening the Collection?'

For a second, everything was confused. There was Nick, so impatient for the answer that he could hardly listen to what Stephen was saying, and Stephen burbling about how they mustn't tell Doug or Mother, so how were they going to get into the Collection room. Hannah felt so irritated that she could have banged their heads together.

And then, as smoothly as two cogs engaging, the two annoyances came together to make one simple solution.

'Listen,' she said, cutting in on both of them. 'Hush.'

They stopped and stared at her and she lowered her voice before she spoke.

'This is supposed to be a secret, right? And Stephen and I can't really think of an excuse to keep going across, if we're not allowed to say I'm mending the automatons.'

'It can't be *that* difficult,' Nick said, sounding almost cross. 'After all, it *is* the same house.'

'Yes but—' Stephen began.

Hannah kicked his ankle. No point in getting into explanations like that, when there was a simple answer staring them in the face. Especially when the whole idea of opening the Collection had started with Nick.

'*You're* the one with the perfect excuse,' she said to him. 'You're studying Samuel Roscoe, and no one'll think it's peculiar if you want to make a catalogue of his automatons. Or—' she took a deep breath and looked triumphantly at both of them '—if you want *us* to make a catalogue of them

44

while you get on with the papers in the library.'

Nick got it at once. Grinned all over his face and clapped her on the back. 'Brilliant!'

But Stephen was still looking unhappy. 'Yes, but why has it *got* to be secret? I don't like that.'

'For heaven's sake!' said Hannah. 'You know Uncle Ernest's senile. He doesn't know what he's saying half the time.'

'So how could he give us permission to do anything?' Stephen frowned.

'Don't you *want* to save this house from falling to bits?' Hannah fixed him with a fierce glare. 'This is the only chance it's got, you know. I don't think the roof can hold out for more than two or three bad winters. After that, the whole place will start being washed away.'

That got to Nick, all right. For a moment, while Stephen was talking, Hannah had been afraid he was going to lose his enthusiasm and start worrying about trouble. But he couldn't stand the thought of his precious Samuel Roscoe's precious house falling into Mapling Beck. Out of the corner of her eye, Hannah saw him shudder.

'How about now?' he said. 'We could go across before I begin work and get it all set up. Then you'll have the rest of the holidays to organize things.'

He was manic. A Samuel Roscoe freak. Even Hannah was knocked for six by the way he hustled them both up the stairs and through the gallery. Polite, apologetic Nick? Huh!

He grabbed the frayed green string hanging from the bell and tugged it so hard that the plastic hook juddered. The bell was still jangling when Doug opened the door.

'Oh, hallo,' Doug said, before anyone could speak. 'Ernest told me you were coming, but he didn't say why.'

That took Hannah's breath away. Uncle Ernest had *remembered*? She found herself wishing that he hadn't, but that was ridiculous, because he did remember some things. Only—why this one?

Nick was talking briskly while she was still thinking. 'I need a catalogue of the automatons in the Collection, and

45

Stephen and Hannah have kindly offered to make it for me.'

'But there's a catalogue already.' Doug looked puzzled.

Nick stared down at his shoes. 'But this is a special catalogue. For the research I'm doing.'

'I suppose it's all right,' Doug said doubtfully, 'if Ernest's agreed. But I don't know why you didn't ask me to ask him.'

He shot a hurt, accusing glance at Stephen. The two of them must have met up earlier on, and Doug's feelings were hurt because he hadn't been let in on what was happening. For a moment Hannah felt guilty, but she brushed it aside. They *couldn't* tell him.

'Can we go downstairs then?' she said.

Doug stepped out of their way. 'Want me to come?'

'No, that's all right,' Hannah said, as kindly as she could.

'We really don't want to cause you any bother,' added Nick. 'If you could just let us in when we want to come—?'

Doug still loitered. Not nosy, exactly, Hannah understood that. It must be hard for him to see them making plans with Nick, shutting him out of them. And he could easily have joined in, if it weren't for Uncle Ernest's dotty idea about keeping things secret. It was just the sort of thing that Doug enjoyed. Fiddling around with machines and making grand schemes for improving the house. It would have been so simple, to smile at him and ask him along. And it would have been good for Stephen, too, to see Doug when he was at ease, enjoying himself.

But they couldn't take the chance. If they disobeyed Uncle Ernest, he was quite capable of squashing the whole scheme flat. Hannah blacked out her mental picture of Doug and Stephen and herself cheerfully undoing screws and oiling joints, and set off along the corridor before anything disastrous could happen.

'Well,' she said as she pushed open the door of the Collection room, 'I know what I'm going to do, for a start.'

Those thick, mustard-coloured curtains got her down. What this place needed was daylight and fresh air. Marching down the room, she tugged at the heavy velvet, ignoring the dust that billowed up. But outside the rhododendrons had grown close to the window, hiding the sky.

'Those'll have to be cleared, won't they?' She turned briskly. What an idiot she was not to have brought her toolbox with her. She was itching to get down to work on the automatons, but she wouldn't really be able to do anything this morning. Just work out which of them were all right and which needed cleaning or mending.

Stephen and Nick were standing on the far side of the table, looking useless.

'Do you want us to do something?' Nick waved a hand at the first cabinet.

'No,' Hannah said. As she pulled the covering cloth off the cabinet, her mind was already starting to take stock. The elephant and the donkey were fine. And the squirrel. But there was a dancing bear in there that Doug hadn't wound up. And a snake. Apart from those—

'You don't want us to help you sort out the automatons?' Stephen came up beside her and peered through the glass. 'There's nothing else we can do, after all.'

'*Nothing else?*' Hannah almost squawked it at him. 'What about the back drive, then? There's no point in me sorting out these jolly little things if no one can get at them.'

'But we haven't got any tools,' Stephen said.

'I think—' Nick blushed. 'I mean, I just happened to notice a pair of shears in the gun room. Do you think anyone would mind if we borrowed those?'

'Great idea.' Hannah didn't really know whether Doug would mind or not, but she wasn't going to get tangled up asking. 'Are you going to give Stephen a hand?'

'I might as well. Just for a bit. But I'll have to go and do some work soon—'

He went on twittering for a moment or two, but Hannah hardly heard, because she was too busy starting her list again. The bear. The snake. And the cow with the crumpled horn . . .

Chapter 5

By the time Stephen had fetched the shears, Nick was outside, standing on the semi-circle of weedy gravel and looking around. Rhododendrons and spotted laurels had grown all the way round the edge to form an almost solid wall. The only break was on the left, where a narrow opening gave just enough space for one person to walk through.

'That can't be the back drive,' Nick said in a puzzled voice. 'The back drive runs down to the bottom road, doesn't it?'

Stephen nodded. 'It comes out at the Lion Gates. You can see them if you walk along the road.'

'So what's this path here?'

Stephen thought for a second. 'It must be the path up to the bridge. It's overgrown on our side, but I think Doug keeps this one clear. He goes up there sometimes.'

Standing in the moonlight, staring over the waterfall at the house below. Watching. A still, black figure against the sky. Stephen pushed the picture out of his mind.

Nick was gazing at the path. 'There must be a good view of the house from that bridge. Could we go up there some time?'

'Now, if you like,' Stephen said eagerly.

Nick gave him an odd look. 'Don't you think we ought to get started on clearing the drive? I thought you'd be itching to begin.' He walked slowly round the edge of the gravel, looking for any signs that there had once been an opening. 'Here?' He pointed to a tangle of rhododendrons.

There was no path at all between them. The rhododendrons grew thickly all the way across, with a skirt of weeds

48

masking them in front, where it was light. But, looking up, Stephen could see a space between the tall trees, like a corridor of air running over the tops of the bushes.

Nick studied it. 'How long since the drive was cleared?'

'A long time.' Stephen frowned, trying to remember. 'I know Mother said once that it was completely overgrown when we got here. That was nine years ago, but I don't think anyone had touched it for years before that. Since the nineteen fifties at least.'

'Hmm.' Nick stared into the bushes for a moment. Then he looked sideways at Stephen. 'It sounds like a pretty impossible job.'

'Yes.' Inexplicably, Stephen felt like laughing with relief. 'Do you think we should go and tell Hannah—?'

'Tell *Hannah*?' Nick pulled a terrified face. 'She'd scalp us alive. No, we'll have to try, at least. Pass us the machete, Carruthers.'

'What?' Stephen blinked, and Nick looked embarrassed.

'Sorry. I was getting carried away there. But this is such a fantastic place for playing jungle games. I bet you and Hannah had a wonderful time here when you were younger.'

Stephen tried to imagine the sort of childhood that Nick was talking about. 'We've never played games much,' he said at last. 'Only draughts and things like that.'

'But—' Nick seemed lost for words. To cover his confusion, he took the shears and waved them dramatically. 'Lion Gates, here we come!'

He began to chop wildly at the nearest branches, snipping off useless little twigs and bouncing the blades off thick, woody branches.

'Let me—' Stephen began, trying not to shudder.

'No, no, it's good for me.' Nick gave the shears another dangerous wave. 'I spend too much time sitting around on my backside.'

Hack, hack, hack. And they were only two or three inches further on. The bushes must be growing faster than Nick was cutting. A hundred years from now, their skeletons would be discovered in the middle of a dense thicket, one brandishing a pair of rusty shears . . .

Stephen couldn't watch. Cutting away undergrowth was almost second nature to him. And to Hannah. For years it had been their first job as soon as they got home for the holidays. Mother virtually met them off the train and pushed the shears and the sickle into their hands. The sight of Nick wasting all his energy and blunting the shears was too much to put up with.

'I—er—I think I'll go for a little stroll round. Call if you want me.'

'Mmm.' Nick hardly took any notice. He was enjoying himself too much.

Stephen left him to it and walked across the gravel to the little path on the other side. No mistake about it. That was kept well-cleared. He could see the raw ends where Doug must have snipped a few encroaching branches in the last day or two. There. And there and there.

Idly he wandered up the narrow, eroded path. It was treacherous underfoot. Dusty and uneven, with loose stones that clattered away from his feet as he climbed. And Doug climbed it in the dark. Came up here when it must be impossible to see the ground, night after night, in the only free time he had, when Uncle Ernest was asleep.

And for what? All he did when he reached the top—all he could do—was stand and look down at the house where the rest of them were getting ready for bed. Nothing to see except lights and closed curtains.

Don't think about it. Stephen screwed up his eyes and pushed his hands down angrily into his pockets. *Don't think—*

The fingers of his right hand met metal. Closed round a thin, hard shape, looped at one end. For a second he was bewildered, and then he remembered the key that Uncle Ernest had given him. He pulled it out and looked curiously at it, as though just by studying the shape of it he could work out what it was for. And somehow it did seem familiar. It was different from the keys that belonged to the inside doors of the house which were all similar, of a standard pattern. But it was too small for the key to an outside door and too big for a desk key.

And yet—he had seen it before, had held it even. Once. Somewhere. And it had unlocked . . . had unlocked . . .

His brain struggled after an answer, reaching into darkness, into uncertainty for a moment. Then there was a gust of wind that set the bushes round him whispering and chattering and broke his concentration. His mind faltered, clamped shut. *No, I don't remember. I can't remember.* He pushed the key fiercely back into his pocket and began to run down the path again, his feet slithering on the loose surface.

As he came out on to the gravel, he caught at a bush to steady himself and, as he did so, his eye was distracted by a movement somewhere high up, inside the house. A face? A flapping curtain? He scanned the windows, trying to find it, but they were all blank.

Just as he was going to turn away, it came again. A curtain moved on the first floor. Twitched aside, deliberately, to show the face that was staring down at him with yellow, bloodshot eyes. For one mesmerized moment, Stephen felt that everything about him was visible, that Uncle Ernest had seen what he did as he climbed the path. And what he thought.

Don't be ridiculous. He forced himself to look directly at the window, to smile and wave politely. But the only answer he got was another movement as the curtain dropped back and Uncle Ernest vanished. Feeling slightly shaky, Stephen walked over the gravel to see how Nick was getting on.

To begin with, he could not see him at all. In fact, he thought that Nick must have given up and gone off to work in the library. But then he heard the faint, unmistakable *clip clip clip* of the shears. Further away than he had expected. He took a few steps into the opening of the drive and looked down it.

Nick was ten or fifteen yards ahead of him, still cutting away with the same vigorous, inefficient strokes. He had taken off his tee-shirt and his back was glistening with sweat, but—could he really have cleared ten yards of thick, close undergrowth already? Stephen looked at his watch. No, it was impossible.

As he walked down the drive, Nick heard him coming and glanced over his shoulder, grinning. 'Pretty good, eh?'

'Unbelievable,' Stephen said truthfully.

Nick pulled a rueful face. 'I knew I wouldn't impress you. It's quite thin growth really. It was only those first few yards that were dense. Must have been something to do with the light.'

And then, of course, Stephen saw that it was true. The branches in front of them were not woody but soft and green and they barely met across the path. Nothing like the impenetrable tangle he had been expecting.

'It's a piece of luck, isn't it?' Nick said cheerfully. 'You should easily be able to get it clear before the end of your holiday now. Relieved?'

Stephen mumbled something vague and went on staring at the bushes. They couldn't be like that. They *couldn't*. They had been growing for thirty years.

'Of course it's obviously been cleared more recently than we knew,' Nick said, eerily echoing his thought. 'Certainly within the last ten years.'

'But it hasn't,' said Stephen. 'It *hasn't*.'

It was only when he saw Nick looking at him with a faintly puzzled expression that he realized how fiercely he had spoken.

As Hannah reached into the third cabinet, her hand knocked a soldier with a sword. It toppled forwards off the shelf and as she caught it in her other hand the sword jabbed her. Actually punctured her skin.

Clumsy fool. She must be cracking up if she couldn't even pick things up without dropping them all over the place. It was a good thing she hadn't brought any tools with her if that was the kind of day she was having. Sucking the ball of her thumb, she moved over to the table with the soldier.

There didn't seem to be anything wrong with it. When she wound the key sticking out of the back of the scarlet coat, it began to strut and brandish its sword. *Very* realistic, thought Hannah sourly, noticing a smear of her own blood on the tip. Perhaps it was actually designed to cut the hand that wound it.

Meant to wound the hand that wound it.

Wince. She must definitely be cracking up if she'd started making puns like that. The automatons had driven her out of her mind, flapping and prancing and waving their arms at her, like something out of a horror film.

And perhaps that wasn't such a joke after all. The room oppressed her. Too many faces. Too many *eyes*. Painted eyes, enamelled eyes, ruby and emerald and turquoise eyes, all peering at her from the shelves of the cabinets and the top of the table.

Worst of all were the eyes of the monks, painted round the walls, peeping at her from under the shadows of their hoods, sly and secretive. *Art!* thought Hannah in disgust. It always had given her the creeps. Stupid, self-indulgent waste of time and money. Give her a nice, complicated machine any day. Something you could work away at until you understood it completely.

And that was it, of course. She wasn't really cracking up. She was just bored with all these silly little automatons. The people who made them had taken a lot of trouble with the outsides, but even without taking them to pieces she could tell that the mechanisms were pretty ordinary. Dull. Surely it ought to be possible to do something a bit more exciting with clockwork. Idly she wondered if there was anything more interesting about that one Nick had wanted to see. What was it?

The French Terror.

She struggled to remember exactly what Nick had said. *Old Sam raved about it . . . paid a few thousand pounds for it and reckoned he'd got a bargain.* None of the automatons here were in that sort of league. It was a pity it had been . . .

Then she remembered Doug's eyes, flickering towards the locked door that led through to the billiard room. Odd, that had been. Something peculiar about his expression. She wished she could have a look through the door. If only it had a fanlight above it, like the door into the Collection

room, she would have stood on a chair to take a peep, but—
'Moron!'

She said it out loud, banging her hand down on the edge of the table and knocking over the little soldier. He tumbled on to his side and lay there with his legs working uselessly, backwards and forwards, backwards and forwards, but Hannah did not even notice. She was already on her way out of the room.

Of course there was no fanlight over the little interconnecting door. But there almost certainly *was* one over the main billiard room door that opened off the lobby. It was sure to match the other doorways that—

Yes. It did.

She tried the doorhandle quickly, just to be certain, but she wasn't surprised that the door was locked. No point in locking one and leaving the other. Anyway, all she wanted was a quick look. Carefully, not making any noise, she carried a chair from the gun room, putting it down gently so that it would not make a sound. Then she kicked off her shoes, climbed on to the padded, embroidered seat and stood on tiptoe, gripping the top of the door frame. She could just see into the billiard room. But there was no sign of a billiard table.

Packing cases. That was her first thought. Big wooden shapes, one long and low, and one tall and thin, like a wardrobe rising from the far end of the flat one. Huge boxes, filling the centre of the big room.

Then she looked a bit more, and her brain began to get to work. No, not packing cases. The wood was much too good for that—dark and polished, each piece carefully shaped. The flat base was like a stage, eight or ten feet long. The tall shape at the end had doors facing the stage. Well-fitting, handleless doors. Tightly closed.

Near the other end of the stage was a second structure. Some sort of framework, much flimsier than the wardrobe shape. But it was exactly level with Hannah and however she craned her head she couldn't get a proper look at it.

All very frustrating. If she had been ten years younger she would have stamped up and down the lobby and kicked the door. Now all she could do was shrug and climb off the chair. Never mind. This afternoon she would be able to come back with her tools and start working on the automatons. Even if they were only dull, simple clockwork. At least she would be getting the Collection ready to go on show. Doing something with some point to it.

She allowed herself one last rattle at the door. But there was no mistake. It was firmly locked, like the other one. And there was no sign of a key for either of them.

Chapter 6

Mother gave them two days before she made any comment. Twice a day, morning and afternoon, Stephen and Hannah went across to work on the Collection, ostentatiously carrying notebooks and pencil cases. She watched them go and watched them come back, but she never said a word. Not until the third day, at lunchtime.

Stephen could see it coming. It was obvious from the careful way she cut her bread. The precision with which she buttered it and placed her thin slices of cheese on top. One, two, three. But she did not actually speak until she had lifted the bread off her plate. Her voice was very casual.

'Have you got any plans for this afternoon?'

Stephen looked down at his plate. *Here we go*. 'We've still got quite a lot of work to do for Nick. On our catalogue of the automatons.'

Mother's hand stopped halfway to her mouth, with the bread poised in midair. 'Oh?' A delicate question. Spiky. 'I hope Doug isn't getting tired of letting you in.' And then a quick laugh, to show it was a joke. Almost.

'He doesn't mind,' Hannah said cheerfully. Stephen wondered whether she had missed all the prickles. 'We're helping him as well.'

Mrs Roscoe arched an eyebrow and tilted her head.

Hannah nodded. 'It's very overgrown out the back there. We're cutting back the rhododendrons.'

'Ah.' Mrs Roscoe relaxed slightly. 'I wondered how Stephen was managing to get his shoes so dirty *inside* the house.'

'Nick's giving us a hand too,' Hannah went on blithely.

'He says it's restful when he's done a lot of work in the library.'

That was a mistake. Stephen knew exactly what would come next, and he was not wrong. Mother stopped relaxing and looked distressed.

'But you should have invited him to lunch if he's helping you.' She waved her hand at the remains of the loaf and the small slab of cheese. 'We could easily have had something more suitable.'

She would have done it, too. Cooked tonight's meal and pretended that it was just a little snack that they had in the middle of the day. Then spent the whole evening commenting on Nick's *healthy appetite* while they ate their bread and cheese.

'Nick always brings sandwiches,' Stephen said. 'He says he likes to work and eat at the same time.'

'Jolly good idea too.' Hannah popped her last piece of bread into her mouth and wiped away the crumbs with her table-napkin. 'Why don't we do the same? It would save a lot of bother.'

That was a bad move. They might only be eating bread and cheese, but they had to eat it 'properly', at the long, polished table in the dining room. With the worn silver cutlery and a starched linen table cloth.

They wheeled it all from the kitchen, on heavy trolleys that had been modern a hundred years ago, and when they had finished their bread and cheese they wheeled it all back again. Washed up the silver carefully and put it in the plate safe in the butler's pantry. Folded up the linen table-cloth after inspecting it for marks. (And woe betide anyone who spilt anything on it. It took three days at least to wash and starch and dry and iron one of those enormous cloths.) Then the water glasses had to be rinsed in three changes of water and dried carefully and the Royal Worcester plates had to be washed up and taken to the china closet. An hour of preparation and clearing up for a meal that couldn't be spun out for longer than twenty minutes.

Mrs Roscoe pinched her lips together and shook her head at Hannah.

'You're both growing. You need to eat properly and give yourselves time to digest. And I really think Mr Honeyball should—'

'How about if he comes to tea?' Stephen put in, before she could insist on anything else. Tea ought to be simple enough.

He got a faint frown for interrupting, but Mrs Roscoe nodded. 'Invite him for tomorrow. A good idea, Stephen. He seems to be working very—thoroughly in the library.' She stood up and began to clear the lunch things on to the trolley. 'It's good to see the library being used for its proper purpose. Libraries don't look lived-in if they're too tidy.' Taking a small, soft brush from the top of the trolley, she brushed the crumbs off the cloth into her hand, with short, sharp strokes.

So Nick had made an untidy mess in the library, had he? Stephen felt like groaning as he stood up, automatically, and took one end of the table-cloth. Even someone as inoffensive as that couldn't do things right.

He and Hannah spread the cloth, inspected it and folded it neatly to put away in the sideboard. Then Stephen turned to push the trolley out to the kitchen. He was washing up today and Hannah was drying.

'Oh, don't you bother with that.' Mrs Roscoe caught at the handle of the trolley and whisked it out of reach. 'You two have got *far* too much to do if you're cutting rhododendrons for Doug as well as doing that catalogue.'

'We've got time to wash up first,' Hannah said. But rather wearily, as though she knew it was no use.

'No, no. I'll do it.' Mrs Roscoe pushed the trolley towards the door that led into the service corridor. 'Don't you worry about me.'

She paused for a moment, looking unselfish, and then disappeared through the door. Stephen felt the familiar inward cringe of guilt.

'Do you think we should go and help?'

'No I don't!' Hannah aimed a kick at one of the bulbous, carved table legs. 'Serve her right if it takes her the whole afternoon. I can't bear it when she's like that. If she hates us going over to Uncle Ernest's side of the house, why doesn't she *say* so?'

'She never said anything about that.' Stephen was trying to be fair. 'We don't *know* that she hates it.'

Hannah looked at him. 'Wouldn't you? If you were her?'

No need to answer that. They both knew exactly how she felt. Stephen looked down at the floor, following the pattern on the carpet. 'She does the best she can. She tries not to let it show.'

'Huh!' Hannah's snort was more miserable than angry. 'I wish she *would* let it show. It would be a whole lot more honest than pussy-footing round just so that we can live here and cadge our school fees off Uncle Ernest. I'd rather have a good row and get out of here, even if it meant going to ordinary schools and living in some beastly flat.'

Leave? Leave school? Stephen felt himself beginning to panic at the very idea. If he didn't know that he could get away at the end of the holidays, go back to Lamplugh and forget everything except Maths and rugby—

'Mother's given up a lot to make sure we can go to decent schools,' he said desperately. 'She cares about our education.'

'Oh nonsense!' Hannah pulled a face. 'It's just snobbery, that's all. We'd be perfectly O.K. if we went to schools like everyone else's—'

And then, miraculously, Mother's footsteps came back down the corridor, her heels clacking on the red stone tiles, and Hannah had to stop. Mother pushed the door open and stuck her head round it.

'Ah, you're still there. Well, if you're not in *too* much of a hurry—'

'Yes?' Stephen said.

'It would be nice of you to make Mr Honeyball a cup of coffee. He refused one this morning, but he sometimes likes one in the afternoon. He might like a slice or two of bread and butter to go with it. And an apple.'

'He brings his own lunch,' Hannah muttered sulkily.

Mrs Roscoe took no notice. 'It will be better on a tray, of course, so that he doesn't need to worry about crumbs. Oh, and a napkin. And one of the Crown Derby cups and saucers.'

'Yes, Mother,' Stephen said patiently.

'But only if you've got time, of course.'

'We've got time.'

'I don't suppose Mr Honeyball will take very long to drink a cup of coffee. But if you can't wait to bring the things back to the kitchen afterwards, just tell me. I can easily—'

'We'll wait,' Stephen said. 'It's all right.'

'Thank you.' Mrs Roscoe smiled at them both. 'Go straight off to do what you're doing afterwards, won't you?' She disappeared again.

Hannah screwed her fists up. 'Yes we bloody well will go straight off. We'll just about have time to walk through the gallery and back, won't we?'

Just the sight of her angry, obstinate face made Stephen's chest tighten. 'Don't—'

'Why *not?*' Now she was angry with him. 'She may be doing the washing up, but she's made certain we don't get over to the other side any earlier. Getting all those bits together and then waiting for the cup and things will probably take longer. And she's made you feel guilty as well. Well *I'm* not going to feel guilty.'

Stephen sighed. 'All right. Don't worry. You go back to the Collection and get on with what you're doing. I can easily—'

'Oh stop it!' Hannah snapped. 'Now you're doing it too. You're as bad as she is.'

She wrenched open the door and stamped off towards the china closet.

Stephen was so *wet*. So totally spineless and servile and *scared*. Hannah worked the knife backwards and forwards in the butter to soften it. One word from Mother and he was falling over himself to please her, when anyone could see that that was impossible. When she was in an injured mood, she would go on being injured whatever you did. If only

Stephen would argue. If only he would say what he thought. But he just went on playing the stupid games that Mother played. That they all played.

And I'm as bad as the rest of them. Gloomily Hannah spread butter over the surface of the loaf and then picked up the bread knife to cut it, slicing paper-thin. However many times she resolved to speak her mind, she never quite got the words out into the open.

'Ready?' Stephen carried the tray across and put it on the table beside her.

It was perfect, of course. The sugar tongs neatly in the sugar, the coffee in the small coffee pot and the hot milk in the jug. Just as if Mother had done it. Hannah felt like spitting in the sugar basin. All that energy just to make a cup of coffee for someone who probably didn't even want it.

As if by accident, Mother appeared in the doorway as they came out of the pantry. Of course. She glanced at the tray and gave it a quick nod.

If she tries to blackmail us into doing anything else, thought Hannah, *I'll scream and shout and—*

Mrs Roscoe held out her hands. 'I can easily take that. If you're in a hurry.'

'We said we'd do it,' Hannah muttered. And pushed past, up the corridor, before Mother had time for a gentle, incredibly tactful hint about manners. Might as well get the stupid business over with.

Stephen knocked on the library door and pushed it open, and she heard him gasp. Not surprising, either. Nick had certainly made a mess of the room. There were piles of papers and photographs all over the desk top, all over the wide windowsills and all over the floor. Nick himself was up at the far end of the room, kneeling in front of yet another overflowing box file.

'We've brought you some coffee,' Stephen said faintly.

'What?' Nick blinked as he looked up.

Hannah knew that look. Knew exactly how maddening it was to have people coming crashing in on you when you were deep in a piece of complicated work.

'Mother thought you'd like some coffee,' she said gently.

61

'Oh yes. Lovely. Thank you.' Nick glanced round with an apologetic frown. 'I'm afraid it's all rather a mess, but your mother said I should make myself at home, and really I need to use all the surfaces.'

Stephen looked helplessly at the overflowing desk. 'Can we just move a few of the papers and—?'

'No!' Nick almost shrieked it. He jumped up and came scurrying down the room towards them, weaving carefully in between the piles on the floor. 'That would be a disaster. I've spent days sorting them into different years. Everything's such a muddle that I can't even begin work until I've done that.'

He took the tray from Stephen and it was his turn to look round helplessly. 'All right if I put it on the floor?' he said at last.

Hannah saw Stephen blench as he looked at the Crown Derby cup and saucer. He was right, too. If they got broken, it would be months before Mother let them forget it.

'Why don't you drink the coffee straight away?' she said helpfully. 'While I hold the tray. Then we can get out of here and leave you in peace.' *And I can get back to my own work.*

Nick looked at her as though she had just worked a miracle, and handed over the tray. Then he poured himself a cup of coffee. 'It's really kind of your mother. I told her not to bother—'

'It's no trouble,' Stephen said.

Hannah gave him a look that showed what she thought of *that*. And then went red as Nick glanced up and caught her at it. Oh dear. Now he would start apologizing all over again.

But he didn't. He gulped down the coffee, swallowed the bread and butter in a couple of bites and grinned at her. 'How's it going? With the automatons?'

Hannah shrugged. 'O.K. There's nothing difficult about them. Very clever and well made, but the mechanisms are pretty standard. I wish that French Terror thing was still around. That must have been a bit more special, mustn't it?'

'Oh yes.' Nick laughed suddenly and slapped himself on the head. 'I'm sorry. I was so busy working when you came in that I forgot I had something to show you. I've found a photograph of it.'

'You have?' Hannah looked round as though she expected it to bounce up at her from the nearest pile. 'Where is it?'

'Over there. On the desk.'

Stephen was standing right beside the desk. Hannah looked impatiently at him. 'Go on. Find it. I can't do anything with this tray.'

'I—'

What was the *matter* with him? He was just standing there looking down at the papers on the table as though he thought they would burn him if he touched them. Hannah couldn't bear to look at him.

'Oh go on, take this.' She shoved the tray at him. 'I'll find it.' She began raking through the heap of papers at the front of the desk.

'No, not there.' Nick stepped round two untidy piles and over the top of a third. 'It's in this lot. The ones I haven't got a date for.'

His hand went straight to it, as if he had a super-efficient filing system there instead of a crazy mess.

'You see? Isn't that interesting?' He flapped the photograph under Stephen's nose. 'It shows that it really did work.'

The coffee pot on the tray gave a sudden shudder. Avoiding Hannah's eyes, Stephen put the tray down under the desk and pushed his hands into his pockets.

'They could have rigged the photograph,' he said, barely glancing at it.

'But that's Samuel Roscoe there, with the beard.' Nick sounded quite shocked. 'He wouldn't have done anything like that. He was the most honest person—'

'For heaven's sake!' If he was going to start drooling about Samuel Roscoe, he'd never stop. Hannah could see the words scrawled on the back of the picture—*The French Terror*—but she couldn't edge round to look at the front without kicking over at least two piles of papers on the floor. 'Can I see?'

'Oh yes. Of course. Sorry.' Nick had a last glance. 'I ought to be able to date it by the clothes, really. Probably around nineteen ten or so. The old man died in nineteen twelve.'

'*Nick!*'

He was almost pressing his nose against the picture now as he studied the details. 'Of course, it's hard to tell about these country places because the people were always behind the London fashions. What do you think, Stephen?' He held the photograph out for Stephen to look at again.

'What's the use of showing him? He won't know. Why won't you let me *see*?'

Hannah felt like jumping up and down with rage and hammering her fists on the desk. With a great effort, she managed to keep still. 'Please, Nick, will you let me have a look at that picture?' she said slowly.

'What do you think, Stephen?' Nick said again.

Stephen looked utterly bewildered, but Hannah suddenly got it. And felt a total idiot for not having realized before that she was being teased. She gave a sudden, loud growl.

'Nicholas Honeyball, if you don't hand over that silly little photograph AT ONCE, I shall run round the library and knock all your heaps of paper into one big jumble!'

Stephen opened his eyes very wide, shocked, but Nick grinned and pretended to shudder.

'No, no, anything but that. Here you are, sir.' He flicked the picture across at her so that it fell to the ground and she had to bend over to pick it up. While she was still stooping, she turned it the right way round.

And it knocked the breath out of her.

She had been assuming that the French Terror was something small, like the other automatons. Something you could stand on a table. But the thing in the photograph was vast. The figure was as big as the people watching. It stood facing the camera, on a low stage. In front of it was the unmistakable shape of a guillotine. A tall framework with a diagonal blade suspended at the top. Much flimsier than the wardrobe shape which stood with open doors at the other end of the stage.

'Not very fit, are you?' Nick said it jokingly, hearing her gasp as she straightened. But then he must have seen something peculiar about her face, because he took a step towards her and put a hand on her arm. 'Hannah? Are you O.K.?'

'Yes, of course I am.' *Calm down, now. Check your facts before you get excited.* She waved the photograph casually. 'I didn't know automatons could be this sort of size. Are you sure this really *is* the French Terror?'

'Oh yes.' Nick nodded. 'Some of the most famous automatons are life-size. Like the Jaquet-Droz writer that can write any short message that you programme into it. With pen and ink. And the silver swan at the Bowes Museum that catches fish in its beak. That was why old Sam got so excited about the French Terror, I think. Because it was one of the really classy automatons. Eighteenth century.'

'But—' Hannah frowned. She didn't know much French history, but surely the French Terror was the French Revolution. And surely that had been—

'That's right.' Nick nodded. 'French Revolution, seventeen eighty-nine. Someone was making that amusing toy there more or less while real live people were having their heads chopped off by the guillotine.' He pulled a face. 'Pretty disgusting when you come to think about it.'

Stephen had gone very pale, but Hannah didn't have time to wonder where he got his delicate feelings from all of a sudden. She put the photograph down on the desk, where they could all see it, and took a deep breath.

'If that's the French Terror, then I know where it is.'

'Where?' It was Stephen who asked, in a quick, breathless voice.

'In the billiard room.' Hannah pulled a face. '*Locked* in the billiard room. I saw it through the fanlight.'

'Oh,' said Nick. And then, more softly, '*Oh!* D'you think we could ask—?'

Stephen stiffened visibly, pushing his hands further down into his pockets. Hannah felt more like weeping tears of frustration. *D'you think we could possibly ask—?* What simple, straightforward lives other people led. Where you could ask someone to do something for you without being beholden and upsetting the whole balance of things.

'If you were really making a catalogue for me,' Nick said persuasively, 'you would need a look at the French Terror. And your great-uncle seems quite happy for me to poke about.'

He was looking expectantly at them both. It seemed cruel to say no, but Hannah couldn't bear the idea of having to go to Doug, to admit that she had been snooping about and to ask him for a favour. And it was even worse trying to imagine what Mother would say if she found out.

Hannah looked down at her feet. 'It's not very easy for us to—'

'Oh, I didn't mean *that*.' Nick shook his head. 'I'll go and ask if you think it's all right.'

It was so simple that Hannah felt like laughing. Turning her back on Stephen, she grinned at Nick. 'Of course you can ask. If you don't mind.'

'I never mind making a fool of myself. Used to it.' Nick grinned back. 'I'll go and do it now, shall I? Before I lose my nerve.'

He was off without a second thought, loping through the door and leaving it open behind him. Hannah turned back excitedly to Stephen.

'Isn't that fantastic? I really fancy having a look at the French Terror.'

But Stephen was bending down with his back to her, to pick up the tray from underneath the table, and he didn't answer. Trust him to be niggling around with something like that. He never seemed to get excited about anything. Even something really worth getting excited about.

Hannah glanced over at the desk, wanting another look at the photograph, to try and get some idea of how the French Terror worked. But it had gone. It wasn't lying on the desk where she had left it, and it didn't seem to have slipped down on to the floor. She was about to ask Stephen if he knew where it was, when it occurred to her that Nick had probably taken it with him. Instead of speaking, she reached out and grabbed the tray from Stephen as he stood up with it.

'Let's get this washing up done. Then we can go and see how Nick's got on.'

'I'll do it,' Stephen said quickly.

Hannah felt like throwing the tray at him. 'Oh don't start being martyred again! We'll *both* do it.'

And she marched off with the tray before he could argue.

Chapter 7

He couldn't get rid of her. When he tried to go off on his own to do the washing up, she nearly threw a fit. Insisted on coming with him, and talked all the time she was drying up, so that he couldn't even think. And the moment they finished, she hustled him away to the gallery before Mother could find them and think of something else for them to do.

Push off, Hannah! Leave me alone! Stop bossing me around! The words sounded good in his mind, and he wished he could yell them at her. That would give her a shock. But he could never shout, any more than Mother could, and he followed her meekly across to Uncle Ernest's door.

'Don't say anything to Doug,' she hissed in his ear as she pulled the frayed green string to ring the bell. 'We'll just go straight down to the Collection room and see if Nick's there. If he's got the key, I expect he'll be in the billiard room already.'

She was almost hopping around with impatience, wanting to know what had happened, but Stephen couldn't share it. All he wanted was to be on his own, to think things over. But there didn't seem to be any chance of that. The moment Doug opened the door, Hannah was through it, hardly sparing time to say 'Thank you'. Stephen followed with a pale, small smile, avoiding Doug's eyes.

Along the corridor. Down the stairs. If Stephen loitered, even for a second, Hannah peered over her shoulder at him and frowned. She obviously couldn't wait to get into the billiard room and get her hands on the French Terror.

And then they came round the corner at the bottom of the stairs and she stopped dead, her shoulders slumping with disappointment. Coming up beside her, Stephen saw Nick standing on a chair outside the main billiard room door, peering through the fanlight.

'No luck?' Hannah said.

Nick tottered, looked round guiltily and almost fell off the chair. Hannah marched across the lobby towards him.

'What happened? Wouldn't they give you the key?'

'It was a bit odd.' Nick frowned. 'I don't think he liked being asked for it—Doug, I mean—and then when he went to look for it he said he couldn't find it. I'm not sure—'

Stephen's breath caught in his throat. 'I think I'll go down the drive and do some more work,' he said quickly, interrupting. 'If there's nothing new to see here.'

The others hardly heard him. They were starting on a long, boring discussion about Doug and the key and the French Terror. Grabbing the shears out of the gun room, Stephen almost ran out of the house and across to the back drive.

There were yards of it clear by now. It took him several minutes to reach the place where he had stopped at lunchtime. When he did, he put the shears down on the ground, slipped a hand into his pocket and pulled out the photograph of the French Terror.

I must be mad. I must be going mad to take it like that.

It wasn't a very good photograph. A group of people, obviously posed, stood looking at the automaton, their stiff, old-fashioned clothes making them seem not quite real. A man and a woman with a little boy in a sailor suit. A much older man with a beard. Stephen recognized *him* all right. It was Samuel Roscoe himself, looking stern and rather rough, like an old sea captain.

But the photograph was dominated by the automaton itself. The ugly, looming shape of the guillotine and the life-size figure of a man that stood behind it, the face so cleverly modelled that it looked almost real. Almost familiar.

I haven't seen it. I wasn't there. Samuel Roscoe died seventy years before I was born. I've never seen it.

But horrors were moving in his mind. Ghosts and hauntings and figures that walked on their own, reaching out from the stage where they should have been with long, murderous arms . . .

'No!'

He said it suddenly, out loud. Not hysterical, but firm. He didn't believe in ghosts. It was an odd trick of his mind that made him think he had been there when the photograph was taken, that he had stood where the little boy was standing and seen—and seen—

His mind jibbed, refused to go on, and he closed his eyes for a second to get a grip on himself. It was perfectly simple. If the photograph made him feel strange, then it should be destroyed. Once it was gone, he would be all right again.

He ripped it quickly into four pieces and then looked around. It would have been easy enough to throw the pieces into the bushes. A few showers of rain, a few nibbling mice and they would have been unrecognizable. But somehow that didn't seem final enough. He wanted them gone completely. Picking up the shears, he jabbed them into a loose patch of ground beside the path, digging a rough hole.

Part of him wanted to fit the pieces together again before he threw the photograph away. Just for a last look. But he wouldn't let himself. Screwing them fiercely in his hand, he pushed them into the hole, scrabbling the earth over with his fingers and patting it flat.

When he stood up, he felt relieved, almost light-hearted. Ready to cut away at the rhododendrons for hours and hours. But before he could start, there was a voice from behind him.

'Taking a rest already?'

Hannah and Nick were walking down the drive towards him. Stephen forced himself not to look down at the bare earth where he had been digging. Managed to make his voice light and teasing, like Nick's, as he replied.

'At least I *am* working. You two look as though you're out for a stroll.'

Nick grinned sideways at Hannah. 'I'm stopping your sister breaking down the billiard room door. She's getting very discouraged about the whole scheme, so I thought she

70

ought to come and see how you're getting on. Just to cheer her up.'

'It's not bad, is it?' Hannah gave Stephen a nod of approval. 'You've done much more than I expected. How are the blisters?'

Stephen looked down at his hands, saw the mud on them and put them behind his back. 'O.K.'

'Let me have a go.' Hannah held out her hands for the shears. 'Nothing like a bit of hacking to get rid of a bad temper.'

She started the moment she got the shears, not cutting wildly, as Nick had done, but making lots of fast, short, efficient cuts. Snap. Snap. Snap. The jaws of the shears ate into the mess of brambles and rhododendrons in front of her.

Nick watched her for a few seconds without saying anything. Then he looked down and scuffed the ground with his foot. Backwards and forwards, kicking the little stones of the gravel, idly, as though he hardly saw them. Backwards and forwards went his left foot, backwards and forwards.

And then stopped suddenly. He stooped down, towards the patch where the earth was disturbed, reaching out with one hand. Stephen felt as though he was going to suffocate, to choke, to be sick.

But no. Nick's hand moved just to one side, ignoring the bare earth and reaching into a rosette of plantain leaves. It came out holding brown metal. A coin. His fingers folded quickly round it, hiding it.

'Guessing game,' he said cheerfully. 'Here is a coin and a very pretty coin and who can tell what the date of this coin may be?'

'A *coin*?' Stephen said.

'Archaeology lesson number one.' Nick waved the fist with the coin in it. 'People drop money *everywhere*. You find it in Roman drains, in medieval rubbish heaps, in eight-eenth century gardens—everywhere. And who knows how long this particular coin has been lurking beside this drive, waiting to be discovered? Very well then, what am I bid?'

Hannah looked over her shoulder impatiently. 'How can we possibly guess when we don't know anything at all about it?'

An odd expression flickered across Nick's face. 'Game,' he said gently. 'You're only guessing.'

'O.K. I'll guess it's Roman then,' Hannah said, not really bothering, turning straight back to the rhododendrons.

Nick drooped slightly, but Stephen couldn't tell whether he was feeling snubbed or disappointed. Either way, Hannah had been pretty rude. Trying to make up for it, Stephen guessed quickly, trying to sound as though he cared.

'I think it's nineteen ten.'

As soon as he had said it, he felt like biting out his tongue. Why that date? But Nick obviously didn't notice anything peculiar about it. He gave him a teasing smile and shook his head.

'*Just* the sort of safe, conservative guess I would have expected from you, Stephen. I'll bet you're right, as well. But I think I'm going to be a bit more adventurous. I'll guess it's—um—er—' He screwed up his face, concentrating on the silly game as though he really cared about winning. 'I'll guess it's eighteen thirty-five.'

'O.K.,' Stephen said. 'What now?'

'Now I open my hand and we see who is closest.' Nick glanced hopefully at Hannah, but she was still clipping away, not taking any notice of either of them. Giving up, Nick waved the fist at Stephen again. 'Ready?'

Stephen nodded. 'I bet I'm right.'

Slowly and dramatically, Nick opened his fingers to reveal the brown, mud-encrusted coin lying in the palm of his hand. He looked down at it, frowned, rubbed it with a finger and then looked again.

'Well?' Stephen said. 'Do I win?'

'What? Yes, I suppose you do,' Nick said vaguely. 'But it's odd.'

Stephen took a step towards him. 'Why? What's wrong?'

'Nothing's wrong. It's just that it's a much newer coin than I expected. Nineteen seventy two.'

Involuntarily, Stephen clenched his fists. 'It can't be.'

'Why ever not?' That was Hannah. She stopped clipping and turned round to stare at him.

'Because—because—'

Nick helped him out. 'Because we thought this drive hadn't been cleared for over thirty years. And that coin can't have been dropped before nineteen seventy two.'

'So?' Hannah shrugged. 'You're wrong, aren't you. This lot can't have been growing for all that time. It's obviously been cleared in the last ten years. Or less.'

'No!' Stephen said.

Hannah stared at him. 'What's up with you? Why shouldn't it have been cleared?'

Stephen scrabbled for a reason. 'Well, we'd know, wouldn't we?'

'I don't see why.' Hannah shrugged. 'Suppose it was cleared seven or eight years ago? I was away at school and you were too small to know much about anything. Doug could easily have done it.'

'He didn't,' Stephen said stubbornly. It seemed very important to get that established.

'So what about the coin, then?' Hannah looked triumphant and held out her hand for it. When Nick dropped it into her palm, she rubbed the mud away, looked at both sides and nodded. 'Nineteen seventy two.'

'It must have got here some other way, then,' Stephen muttered. 'Perhaps a bird dropped it.'

Yes, that was it. Obvious. He could almost see the bird now, with the coin gripped firmly in its sharp, cruel beak, flying across the tree tops and then, distracted by a prettier treasure, opening its beak to let the coin fall down, through the undergrowth on to the ground beside the drive. Magpies did that sort of thing, didn't they? That must be the explanation. He said it again, to settle it.

'It must have been a bird.'

A *bird*? If Nick hadn't been there, Hannah would have laughed in his face. Why not an elephant? Or a fairy? And why shouldn't the drive have been cleared, anyway? It was pretty stupid the way things were, if you came to think of it. Every time Doug wanted to go into town, or anywhere else, for that matter, he had to come through their part of the house to the front door. She had always assumed that he liked it that way, but it would have made a lot more sense for him to have his own entrance. It was just that Stephen couldn't bear to be wrong about anything.

Oh well, if he wanted to be like that why should she care? She held out the coin to Nick. 'Want it?'

When he shook his head, she tipped it out of her hand on to the ground and brushed her hands together. But the mud was sticky and it smeared right across the palms in a long, dark streak.

'Here, have my handkerchief,' Nick said. 'To wipe off that earth.'

He began to fumble in his pockets, quite ignoring the mud that he was spreading from his own hands on to his jeans. After a second or two, it became obvious that he had actually lost his handkerchief. No one else would have cared, of course, but he looked embarrassed and searched all his pockets again.

'I'm sorry. I know I had one somewhere. Just wait a minute and I'll find it for you—'

Don't bother, Hannah wanted to say, but that seemed rude somehow. She glared at Stephen. 'Haven't you got one?'

He must have been deep in his own thoughts, because he jumped when she spoke to him. 'What? A handkerchief? Oh yes.'

He pulled it out, quickly, and held it out to her. Typical Stephen. She had lost her handkerchief, as usual, but his was still snow-white and neatly folded. As she took it, Hannah wondered if he ever did anything as messy as blowing his nose.

But there was something tangled up in it, something long and thin, lodged in the folds. Hannah tipped it out into her hand and glanced at it.

'What's this key, Stephen?'

74

And he blushed. Stephen, who never showed what he was thinking, went bright red and opened and shut his mouth, lost for words. Hannah looked down again at the key, much more interested now. It looked like the key to a room. It looked—

Her heart jumped so hard that it knocked the breath out of her. It wasn't *possible*. Was it? She looked up, straight at Stephen, glaring at him so that he would have to tell her the truth.

'Where did you get this key from?'

'I—' He seemed to be trying to pull himself together. 'I'd forgotten all about it.'

'O.K., O.K. So now you've been reminded—where did you get it from?'

'Hannah,' Nick said softly. He laid a hand on her arm, but she twitched away.

'Well?'

'Uncle Ernest gave it to me,' Stephen said. 'When I went to ask him about the automatons.'

'And what is it?'

'I don't know. He didn't tell me.'

Hannah gave him another glare, but he met her eyes straight on, so she thought he was probably telling the truth. Slowly she turned the key over in her hand.

'It might be, you know,' Nick said, answering the question she hadn't asked. 'Anyway, there's no reason why we shouldn't go and try, is there?'

'Of course not!' Now he had said it, Hannah could hardly bear to wait. 'Come on. We'll do it now.'

She started back towards the house, with Nick beside her. For the first few yards, she thought Stephen was going to stay behind, but then she heard him coming after them, his feet crunching slowly and reluctantly on the gravel. Well she wasn't going to wait for him. She was going to open the door the moment she got there. *If* the key fitted. It was quite difficult to make herself walk quietly into the house and through the Collection room to the interconnecting door.

But she seemed to have picked up some of Stephen's craziness. When she looked at the lock, her hand began to shake so much that she didn't think she was going to be able to put the key in. It was ridiculous. What was so frightening about opening a locked door? Even if it *was* in Uncle Ernest's part of the house. She knew what was in the room already. All the same, something stopped her and she held the key out to Nick.

'You do it,' she said brightly.

He grinned as he took it from her. 'Be a bit of a let-down if it's the wrong one, won't it?'

But it wasn't the wrong one. As Stephen walked down the room towards them, Nick slid it into the keyhole and twisted his wrist and it turned with a very faint click, as though it had been locked for a long time.

'Here we go then,' said Nick. And he pushed the door open.

Chapter 8

'But it's broken,' Hannah said.

The French Terror was standing in the middle of the billiard room, exactly as it had stood in the photograph. Exactly where Stephen had expected it to be. Its long stage filled the space where the billiard table would have been, and tall, branched candlesticks flanked it on either side, six feet high.

But the stage was empty. No life-size figure gazed out at them from behind the guillotine. And the guillotine itself was damaged. The heavy diagonal blade hung down loosely on one side, sagging away from the black pillar which supported it, and in the front of the pillar was a jagged-edged hole ripped about three feet from the bottom.

Stephen felt his tensed muscles begin to relax. 'You see? Doug said it never worked.'

'That doesn't mean I can't mend it, does it?' Hannah walked through into the billiard room and stood beside the French Terror, staring up at the guillotine. 'But it's weird.'

'What's so peculiar?' Nick followed, leaving Stephen standing on his own, watching them.

'Well—' Hannah frowned and peered behind the broken pillar. 'This all looks so well made. Lovely dark, polished wood. Beautiful joints. Real cabinet-making stuff. But the pillars are rubbish. Just a wooden framework covered with black paper, and they haven't got any back to them at all. You can look in and see the weights that go up and down to balance the guillotine blade. Except that the weight on this side is missing.'

'Perhaps it's been mended before,' said Nick. 'By someone who didn't take a lot of trouble.'

Hannah ran her hand down the side of the pillar and shook her head. 'No, look how they fit into the stage. Nothing bodged up about that. I reckon it's all part of the original thing.'

Stephen stared at the torn edges of the paper and put one elbow against the door frame to steady himself. 'What about the figure in the photograph? Do you think it's behind those doors? In the cupboard thing at the back of the stage?'

He felt very strange. Breathless and dizzy and not quite real. But he wasn't going to give in to that. He forced himself to walk down the billiard room, past Hannah and Nick, until he was level with the cupboard. Before he could start to wonder what was in the darkness on the other side of the doors, he put a hand on the stage and jumped up.

'I'll look, shall I?'

'But it might not be strong enough—' Nick yelped.

At the same moment, Hannah shouted, 'Get down, you idiot! If the stage breaks, you'll go crashing into the works.'

'It's perfectly solid. Like you said.' Stephen tapped a foot on the stage to prove it. Now he was up here, instead of looking at it from the ground, he felt a lot more normal and he scrabbled with his fingernails at the crack between the two doors. 'I don't know if I can get these open. I—oh!'

It took him by surprise. At the back of his mind, he had been thinking that the doors would be locked tight, like all the other doors connected with the French Terror. But they weren't. They flew open easily, at a touch, and Stephen found himself gazing into the eyes of a boy of his own height and around his own age.

For a couple of seconds, the illusion was perfect. The boy had real clothes, real hair, and glass eyes that stared out of the shadows straight at Stephen. Not a stupid, vacant doll-face, but a face that you would swear had once belonged to a living person. A face you could recognize.

Then Hannah broke the spell. 'Hey! That's not the figure that was in the photograph, is it? The plot thickens. What else is there up there? Oh come on, Stephen. Get down so I can have a look.'

That seemed a bit much, seeing that she had told him not

78

to go up there in the first place, but Stephen did not feel up to arguing. He jumped down and let her take his place.

It's just a good model, that's all. I was surprised because I thought it was a real person. That's all. There's absolutely no way I could have recognized that boy, because I don't remember being in this room before or seeing the French Terror or—or anything.

Hannah wasn't wasting any time on eyeball to eyeball confrontations with the boy in the cupboard. She was down on her hands and knees, peering past his legs, in their eighteenth century breeches.

'There are more of them in here!' she called out.

Two more, said Stephen's mind, before he could stop it.

'I can't see exactly, but I think it's a man and a woman.' Hannah's cheek was almost on the surface of the stage. 'Anyway, there are certainly two more pairs of legs in here. One in some sort of trousers and one in a long skirt. They're all standing in a circle, very close, facing outwards.'

Nick tried to peer round the open door. 'Sounds interesting. Do you think they all get chopped?'

'Could be.' Hannah stood up, dusting off her hands. There were soft, grey smears of fluff all over the knees of her jeans. 'It looks as though they're all on some sort of turntable. Let's see if we can get them going.'

She jumped off the stage and prowled round to the back.

'Oh yes, there's a handle here that must be for winding the thing up. And a lever to turn it on. Hang on a second.'

'I'm not sure you ought to—' Nick peeped nervously round the side at her. 'This thing must be pretty valuable, Hannah. Even broken. We ought to be very careful.'

'I *am* being careful,' Hannah said cheerfully. They heard the slow, metallic clicking of clockwork being wound. 'It's hard work. The spring must be gigantic.'

'Don't—I mean it *is* possible to over-wind things.' Nick looked wretched.

'Tell him to shut up, Stephen,' Hannah said, without appearing. 'Tell him what a genius I am with clockwork.'

'She is.' Stephen's voice cracked and he coughed to clear his throat. 'She won't hurt it.'

He wasn't sure whether or not Nick believed him, but a second or two later Hannah called out, 'Right folks, here we go. I'm going to turn it on.'

Stephen's heart gave a huge thud and he stepped backwards.

'Are you all right?' Nick said softly.

But before Stephen could answer, there was a loud grinding, grating noise of metal screaming against metal. Nothing moved visibly but from inside the French Terror the noise went on and on.

'Turn it off,' Nick yelled. 'Quick, before you break it.'

The noise stopped and Hannah stepped out from behind the automaton looking shaken. 'Something very wrong inside there, isn't there?'

'You see? You *see*?' Stephen suddenly found himself talking very fast, the words flooding out almost before he knew what he was going to say. 'It's broken. Doug said it was broken and now you've heard for yourself. There's nothing we can do with it. We'll just have to leave it alone.'

'*Leave it alone?*' Hannah stared at him as though he was mad. 'Of course I'm not going to leave it alone. I'm going to mend it.'

'But you can't.' Stephen whirled round, appealing for support. 'You said it was valuable, didn't you, Nick. *You* said she ought to leave it alone.'

Nick looked miserable and embarrassed. He obviously felt just as bad as Stephen would have done about being involved in someone else's family quarrel. 'You did say that she was good with clockwork.'

'Of course I'm good with clockwork,' Hannah said impatiently. 'Stephen knows that perfectly well. I've been mending things in this house ever since I was ten and some of those are pretty valuable, but no one ever throws a fit about it. Not even Mother.' She grabbed Stephen's shoulder and pulled him round to face her. 'Go on. I'm right, aren't I?'

Stephen looked at her angry, obstinate face and then looked past her, at the polished wooden shape of the French

Terror and the looming framework of the guillotine. 'I think you ought to leave it alone.'

'But *why*?' Hannah gave his shoulder an exasperated shake. 'You must have a reason.'

Of course there must be a reason. It was nonsensical to do anything without a good reason. But Stephen felt that he could not start to think what his reason was. It was the same sort of feeling that he had had at school last term, when he was rowing and the boat overturned. No time to plan or work out the best way to untangle his legs from his oar or attempt to avoid the thrashing limbs all round him. Everything else had been blotted out by the total, over-powering need to get *out*, to get up to the air.

'Don't try to mend it,' he said.

She let go of his shoulder and turned away. 'You're being ridiculous. First you forget all about the key, when you ought to have guessed it would have something to do with the Collection. And now you're trying to stop me doing something you know I'm quite capable of. What's the *matter* with you? Do you know something I don't?'

'There's nothing the matter with me,' Stephen said loudly. 'And I don't know anything. *Nothing*!'

He didn't realize just how loudly he had spoken until Nick and Hannah both stared at him. Then his words replayed themselves inside his head. Too loud, too fast, too emphatic. Especially when he was the sort of person who never raised his voice.

Hannah looked away first. 'Well, you can be peculiar if you want to. I'm going to get my tools and have a look at the works of this machine.'

He mustn't say anything else. He mustn't.

Nick put a hand on Stephen's arm. 'Here,' he said gently. 'What about that bridge you were talking about the other day? You said you'd take me up to see the view sometime. Could we go now?'

Stephen followed him meekly out of the room, not glancing back to see what Hannah was up to.

Thank goodness for that!

Hannah felt as though she would have started screaming if the two of them had stayed around any longer. At the back of her mind, niggling and nasty, was the feeling that something was up with Stephen—but so what? What could she do? If only she could have taken off the top of his head, adjusted his screws, oiled him, she would have done it with pleasure, but that was no use with people. The only thing to do with them when they got het up was to ignore them and let it blow over. He'd be much better off with Nick.

All the same, she felt grumpily annoyed as she went back into the Collection room to fetch her tool bag. Not really the right sort of mood to be working on a delicate, valuable piece of machinery. If she wasn't careful, she would be dropping nuts and bolts and unscrewing things before she had noticed exactly how to replace them.

She walked up and down the billiard room a few times, taking deep breaths and gazing up at the painted ceiling that Nick had been so anxious to see when he first came. Fat, fleshy women sprawled across it, not quite covered by pieces of misty, floating drapery. They would have been disgusting if they hadn't looked so chilly in the damp green light that filtered between the rhododendron leaves.

'Nice woolly vests,' Hannah said out loud. 'That's what you all need.'

The thought quite cheered her up and, once she was sure that her hands were steady, she went round to the back of the French Terror and began to unscrew the beautiful brass screws that held on the rear panel.

It was large and heavy. She had to loosen all the screws and then let it fall forward into her arms. It wasn't easy to manhandle it to the side of the room, but she finally managed to get it propped safely.

Now for the works. The moment she turned to look, she could see that they were in a different class from the tiny, elementary clockwork mechanisms she had been mending for the last couple of days. Nothing mass-produced here. Every part had been perfectly tooled and finished to fit its unique place in this unique automaton. Made to last but, more than that, made perfectly because that was the way that things should be made.

Nothing was as mind-blowingly beautiful as a machine, where hundreds of tiny parts fitted together, precisely, to carry out actions designed by someone not there. Someone who could even be dead. The French Terror's maker had been gone for around two centuries, but if she could mend his machine it would move again, exactly as he had planned. Music or painting couldn't compare with that. Decorative, frivolous things. A machine *meant* something.

Only, of course, the French Terror didn't mean much at the moment. Hannah stopped gazing adoringly at it and remembered the unpleasant graunching noise that had been the only result of turning it on. Metal on metal. Something caught in the works, or some part that had got misplaced.

There was a slow way to find that and a quick way. If she had had all day, she would have begun taking the works to pieces, bit by bit, making notes as she went. But she had only got half an hour or so. And if only she could hear that noise again, she was fairly sure she could guess where it was coming from.

She flicked the lever on the right hand side. *Graunch.* But before the graunch there had been a slight, a very slight movement of the turntable. It ought to be going round. Taking away the boy who was facing out through the cupboard doors and turning another figure to take his place. But it couldn't turn, because something was stopping it. And Hannah was ninety per cent sure that the graunching noise had come from under the turntable.

She could just reach it, by kneeling down on the floor and pushing one arm through the machinery, to the left of the huge, tightly coiled spring. Holding her breath, she reached in as far as she could and slid her fingers round the rim of the turntable and into the narrow space underneath.

There was a rough surface above her knuckles, grooved as though it connected with a cogwheel further round. And in the centre, at the limit of her fingertips' reach, was the central spindle. Hannah screwed up her face, trying to visualize the shape of everything she was touching. It all seemed to make sense so far.

She moved her fingers sideways, to the right of the spindle, and suddenly they were scrabbling at an unexpected shape. Round, like a short cylinder with closed ends. It didn't seem to be joined to anything else, because it rolled freely when she touched it, and it didn't seem to be jamming the works, either. Hannah turned her head away so that she could reach in as far as possible. Gently, with her fingertips, she rolled the cylinder closer, until she could get her hand round it. Then she wriggled backwards, away from the machinery, and sat up to see what she had found.

It was a very old, rusty tin with a dirty label. A tin of baked beans.

Beans? They were old all right, but they were definitely not eighteenth century beans, so what on earth were they doing in the works of an eighteenth century automaton?

Putting the tin down on the floor, she wriggled her arm back into the works and began to feel around again. It only took her a second or two to find another loose tin. Peas this time. She put it beside the beans and went back to try again.

She found five loose tins before she got to the one that was jammed. Two tins of baked beans, one tin of garden peas, one tin of sliced peaches and a tin of spaghetti hoops.

The sixth tin was the one that was jammed. It was in the very centre, tight up against the back of the spindle, and Hannah thought she was going to have to take the whole machine to bits to get it out. But she pushed her arm in as far as it would go, scraping her shoulder on the edge of the huge spring, and gradually wiggled it free by knocking it first one way and then the other. Backwards and forwards it went, backwards and forwards and backwards and forwards and suddenly it was rolling loose like the others. As she closed her hand round it, she could feel something sticky on her fingers. Treacle? Tar?

Blood?

Don't be stupid, Hannah Roscoe! This place is turning you into a hysterical idiot! She pulled the tin out quickly before she could start imagining any other ridiculous things. It was a tin of condensed milk, punctured by the machinery, with a thick, white trail oozing out of it. Hannah was so relieved that she sucked her sticky fingers clean before she noticed how dirty the tin was.

So. Six tins. It was crazy. Why on earth would anyone dump a load of shopping into the French Terror? And once they'd dumped it, why should they leave it there, for years and years, to get old and dusty?

Muttering to herself, Hannah carried the tins round to the far side of the automaton, out of her way, and piled them in a neat pyramid, with the condensed milk on top. She stared at them for a moment or two, but the more she stared the less sense they made. In the end, she shrugged and went back to the French Terror again. Now what would happen when she pulled the lever *this* time?

No graunching noise. For a second she thought she had solved the whole problem by getting the tins out of the works. As she pulled the lever, the turntable began to revolve, creaking slightly as the machinery moved again after being still and unoiled for a long time. Slowly, slowly round, anti-clockwise. The boy moved away from the front and, in his place, came the figure of the woman in her long eighteenth century dress, with her high-piled hair.

The doors at the front opened by themselves, so that the woman was looking out on the stage, towards the guillotine, and Hannah thought breathlessly, *I've done it, I've done it*!

And then—nothing. Just a slight whirring from the works. She waited a full five minutes, but nothing more happened and in the end she had to give in and turn the thing off again. But she was not really disappointed. Not when she thought about it. Taking the tins out of the works was just a peculiar fluke. Now, if she wanted to mend the French Terror properly, she would have to set about understanding it. Which was the interesting part.

Quietly she sat down on the ground at the back and began to stare into the machinery, not poking around or unscrewing anything. Just thinking.

Chapter 9

'I haven't been up here since I was small,' Stephen said as they started to climb the path. 'It's too overgrown to get up on our side now.'

His voice sounded high and tight in his own ears, but how could he be natural? He was so embarrassed that it was an effort to get any words out at all. That was almost a row he had had with Hannah back there, about the French Terror. They hardly ever had rows, so that was disturbing enough. But to have a row in front of Nick, a stranger they'd only just met—that was unbearable. What had he been thinking of, and why had he made such a fuss?

'You can't really see the house properly from anywhere else,' he said, forcing the words out. Pretending that things were normal and there hadn't been a quarrel. 'The trees hide it from people in the valley and there's no way of walking over the hill and looking down on it. I suppose if you had an aeroplane—'

'Stephen,' said Nick.

Stephen stopped and looked round at him and Nick smiled, very gently.

'It's pretty steep up here,' he said. 'Don't bother about the polite conversation. Just save your breath for walking.'

'I—'

'It's O.K.' Nick smiled again. 'I spend the whole time screaming at my two brothers when I'm with them. Even now.'

It was like having his mind read and for a moment Stephen was furious. Fancy talking about it! Crashing in and actually putting it into words, instead of ignoring the whole thing and waiting for it to blow over. It was indecent.

But Nick went on looking at him and all of a sudden something shifted in his mind and he saw that it was all right after all. Because he wasn't being criticized or laughed at or intruded on. Nick was just trying to tell him that it didn't matter.

Stephen grinned back. 'You should see how I beat her up when no one's looking.'

It wasn't quite a convincing joke, but it was enough. After that, they could walk in silence up the dusty, irregular path that wound steeply towards the top of the waterfall. Stephen kept his eyes on the ground and tried not to think about Doug going that way in the darkness.

'It's amazing,' Nick panted, when they were halfway up. 'There's not even a glimpse of the waterfall, is there? The bushes go all the way up to the top. It's extraordinary to think this was just a bare bit of moorland before Samuel Roscoe got to work on it.'

'It must have cost him a fortune,' Stephen said. Samuel Roscoe was a nice, safe subject, better to think about than Doug. Or the French Terror. 'Why did he build it *here*? I mean, why not stay in London?'

'Human nature, isn't it?' Nick stopped for a breather, leaning against a tree trunk, and Stephen waited for him. 'He came back to show he'd made it. To lord it over the people who'd been too grand to speak to him before, like I said the other day.'

'And that was all?' It didn't seem a very good reason for wasting money.

'Well no, I don't think that was *all*.' Nick looked slightly embarrassed, as though he had been asked about his own private feelings. 'I think he actually loved this dale. Not the people, but the place. He wanted to live here, but he wanted to live here with all the mod. cons. and the comforts he would have had in a place like London. So he poured the money in, to pay for every gadget you could think of. And then, when the locals still treated him like a vulgar social climber, he planted this lot round his precious house to stop them sneering at it. Shut himself in with it.'

Stephen felt like shuddering. 'That's creepy.'

'Sad,' Nick said. 'The house took over from the dale in his mind, I think. He loved it more than anything or anyone. By the end he was a bit mad and he just stayed here and wrote long letters to his son about how to succeed in business and how to toughen up *his* son—your Uncle Ernest. So they would be worthy to inherit Roscoe's Leap.'

Toughen up Uncle Ernest? Stephen looked sideways to make sure it hadn't been a joke, but it wasn't. Nick had hardly noticed he was speaking out loud, because he had been so busy thinking about Samuel Roscoe.

'He's very—' Stephen hesitated. 'He's very real to you, isn't he?'

Nick started to climb again, leading the way. 'I think about him all the time,' he said over his shoulder. 'It's uncanny being here, because he's all around, in every room. All just as he planned.'

Walking behind, Stephen tried to imagine it. Nick had spoken as if he could visualize Samuel Roscoe in the house. As if he felt his presence and cared about him. *We're the shadows for him. The ghosts. The people who aren't really in the house.* It was an odd, uncomfortable thought and Stephen spoke again, to get rid of it.

'We're nearly there now.'

The path made one more zigzag and the bridge was ahead of them. Nothing splendid, just an ordinary grey stone arch spanning the stream above the waterfall. The far end of it was blocked by a thicket of bushes that hid the opposite bank, encroaching on to the stonework of the bridge itself.

Beyond the gap.

For as long as Stephen could remember, the bridge had been broken. The middle section had fallen down into the beck and there was a couple of feet of empty air between the two stone curves that stretched out, one from each bank. The nearer half looked solid enough, but the one on the far side was perilously overgrown. Small flowers bloomed along the top of the parapet, growing up out of the mortar, and two rowan trees had pushed their way out along the stones, snaking their roots down through tiny gaps to hunt for earth below. Stephen could see some of them dangling through cracks, hanging in midair above the waterfall.

While he was watching, mortar dust trickled suddenly from one of the cracks for a second or two and dropped in a thin stream down to the pool, like sand in a giant eggtimer. How could Doug come up here night after night and stand on the bridge, even on this side, when there were such clear signs of ruin?

Nick did not hesitate, though. He walked out, nearly to the broken end, and leaned with his arms on the parapet, looking at the house.

'Roscoe's Leap,' he said, and his voice cracked slightly. 'He was a sentimental old devil underneath it all, wasn't he?'

Gingerly, Stephen stepped on to the bridge after him, because it seemed rude to do anything else. The stone felt perfectly firm under his feet, but he couldn't forget the huge drop below, to the sharp, jagged rocks of the waterfall. He didn't take his eyes off the bridge until the moment when he reached Nick's side and turned to look.

'Pure romanticism,' Nick said admiringly and for a second—just a second—Stephen caught his mood and saw what he was seeing. The waterfall crashed splendidly under them, dropping in a white torrent to a deep, black pool. Beyond the pool, spanning the stream as it began to flow downwards again, was the house that Samuel Roscoe had built there by a mixture of fabulous riches and unbeatable stubbornness. Roscoe's Leap.

It arched up over its own downward-arching reflection in the pool, not beautiful but startling, unlikely. The windows of the gallery were green with a mysterious haze, and the pale towers clustered at each end like castles out of a story book, promising witches, princesses, fortune and success. Even the weeds growing in the angles of the roof were part of the illusion, as if the ancient forest was stretching out its fingers to claim back the house, casting a hundred-year sleep over everything.

Only it wasn't an ancient forest. It was an annoying mixture of trees and shrubs that caused Stephen hundreds of blisters every year.

The romantic picture broke up into familiar, weary details. The gallery roof was sagging nastily and there were a couple of cracked windows on the attic floor. Two or three unpleasant, jagged cracks were creeping up the walls on Uncle Ernest's side, breaking the greyish-green coating of dirt that covered the surface of the concrete. Everywhere Stephen looked, he saw something that meant money and hard work and he felt exhausted and angry. Whatever they did, they could never be sure of a sound roof, a dry, clean house. The ordinary, everyday things.

He did not realize he had sighed until Nick looked curiously sideways at him. 'You don't like it?'

'I—' Stephen hesitated just a fraction too long, until it was impossible to answer with a polite lie. He looked down at his feet and immediately Nick was apologetic.

'You mustn't think—I didn't mean to pry.'

'No. No, of course not.' Stephen shrugged. 'It's bound to seem more exciting to you, isn't it? Being a stranger.'

'I hadn't really thought of it as a place to live.' Nick looked down at the house again, and Stephen wondered what he was seeing this time. 'I should think it's pretty cold and damp sometimes, isn't it?'

'It's not so bad in the summer. You get used to it.'

'Have you always lived here?'

Stephen looked down at his fingers, which gripped the stone parapet and a memory nudged at the back of his mind. 'Not always.'

They had arrived once, for the first time, and stood in the shadows under the huge front porch. Hannah had been standing beside his pushchair and he had been sitting in it, holding on to the bar in front of him. Cold, wet metal. And a voice whispering, half-joking. *Are schools really this important?* Mother's voice?

No, it couldn't have been Mother, because he could remember looking up at her as she answered. Could remember exactly the pale, determined set of her face as she hissed the words. *It won't be for long. Only until the old man dies.*

How many years ago was that? Eight? Nine? He had

certainly been no older than four. The memory was very distant, tiny and precise, like an image from a dream. The four of them had stood in the shadows, waiting. Beyond that his mind had kept nothing. Even though he concentrated, he could not bring back any picture of the door opening or anyone welcoming them.

'Stephen?' A hand touched his shoulder. 'Are you all right?' Nick was peering anxiously into his face. 'You look a bit—'

'Sorry, I was thinking.' Stephen shook himself free automatically, moving away from Nick's hand. 'Shall we go down again? It's almost four o'clock. Mother will be expecting me for tea.'

'I hope you have it properly, in the drawing room,' Nick said, teasingly. 'With lots of cucumber sandwiches and fairy cakes and maids in starched caps and aprons.'

That certainly was a joke and Stephen smiled. Pity it wasn't funny. Drawing room tea was exactly the sort of thing Mother would have liked to do.

Then he remembered. 'You can see for yourself tomorrow. I'm supposed to invite you.'

'That's very kind.' Nick looked at his watch. 'In that case, I ought to get back to work. There's a lot to do, and I haven't done a stroke this afternoon.'

He wasn't very good at the polite lie, however hard he tried, because everything showed so clearly on his face. And Stephen could tell that he didn't fancy wasting his time on a tea party.

A total, *total* waste of time, Hannah thought angrily at half past three the next day. Any minute now, she would have to go and brush her hair and put on a dress and pretend that Nick was some kind of super-polite visitor. And all the time, he would be fretting to get back to the library and go on with his work and she would be itching to get back to the French Terror.

Because she had just, that instant, understood how it worked and it was so simple and so deadly that she could feel the skin between her shoulder-blades prickling.

The figures executed *themselves*.

As the doors opened, the figure facing through them moved forward on to the stage, its legs stepping, the concertina'd rod in the centre of its back expanding to let it come away from the spindle to which it was attached. It walked to the guillotine and bent forwards over the block.

And, after a second, bent again, a fraction lower, pressing down on the catch concealed in the block. Crash. That was it. The guillotine blade was released and came rattling down on to the neck beneath, snapping apart the connection that held head to body.

Lay your head on a guillotine and get what you bring down on yourself. Ho, ho, very witty. And the next trick, of course, was to prepare the same disaster for someone else. And they did that too. The severed head disappeared through the floor of the stage, going round on a moving belt to be joined to its neck again behind the scenes. Meanwhile, the headless body backed away, back to the cupboard, raising the guillotine blade for the next victim.

Hannah didn't know whether to admire or shudder. The machinery was elegant and ingenious. Beautifully worked out and fantastically made. Man and woman and boy, going round and round in that circle of death for ever. Coming out, one after another, and stepping into the trap that had been prepared by the one before—which they must spring themselves.

But—had the man whose brain worked out the mechanics of it also devised the gruesome thing that his machine did? Could one mind hold both those things? Hannah thought history was one big yawn, but she had at least heard about the French Revolution and the bloodbath it brought about at the end of the eighteenth century. Not pretty. So what were you supposed to do while you watched this automaton? Laugh? Gloat? It was monstrous.

Or it would have been, if it had worked. But there was one crucial piece missing. The whole heavy machine depended on two weights that hung down inside the hollow guillotine pillars. They counterbalanced the weight of the figures and the weight of the guillotine blade. The left hand weight was there all right, a long brass one, a bit like a sash window weight, hanging from a cord. But the right hand weight had gone.

Good thing too, thought Hannah, shuddering.

And then she stopped, hearing her own thought over again. Was she afraid of a machine? What was happening to her in this room? She was getting as peculiar as Stephen.

The French Terror might have been shocking once. Obscene, even. But now it was just a curiosity and if she could get it mended it would bring tourists flocking in. Thousands and thousands of them. Bringing enough money to mend the roof and fix the plumbing and make the electric wiring safe and—

And all she had to do was find another weight to match the one that was already there. Not exactly a cripplingly difficult job. All she had to do was untie the weight and take it off to weigh on the bathroom scales.

Scrambling up on the stage, she reached through the open back of the left hand pillar and began to undo the knot that held the weight. An awkward, lumpy knot it was too, which surprised her. Everything else was perfectly made, even the flimsy, paper-covered pillars. It was as though this single clumsy knot had been tied by someone else. Oh well, perhaps it had. Two hundred years was a long time.

Working away at the knot, she loosened it gradually and she was able to lift the weight free. It was heavier than she had expected and as she let go of the cord the guillotine blade rattled down on to the block, making her jump. Idiot! What was the matter with her today? She ought to have realized that that would happen.

At least she had the weight. She was halfway to the door with it when she suddenly remembered that she couldn't just walk out with it under her arm. Because of Doug. If he saw that she had started taking the French Terror to bits, he would never believe that she was just making a catalogue for Nick. She'd have to smuggle it out.

But it wasn't the sort of thing you could tuck in your pocket or up your tee-shirt. Hannah looked round for camouflage. It would have to be her toolbag.

She tipped the tools out and hid them on one of the window-seats, behind a closed curtain. The empty bag was just long enough to take the brass weight and Hannah slid it in and did up the zip feeling rather foolish, as though she was playing a baby's game. Right. If she got a move on she would be able to get it weighed before tea.

She was just climbing the stairs when a voice spoke her name.

'Hannah?'

An anxious voice trying to sound offhand. Doug's voice. Hannah swallowed and was annoyed to find that her throat had gone dry. She looked up to the top of the stairs.

'Hallo.'

'How are you getting on with your catalogue? Having fun?'

'I've got a lot of useful work done, thank you.'

Damn Uncle Ernest, she thought suddenly, savagely. It would have been really good to tell Doug about the French Terror. Even ask his advice, perhaps. He might be a bodger, but she'd learnt a lot from him when she was younger and, even now, when they were talking about wires and screws and motors, she could almost forget how things were. Could almost feel that they were still—

But no, she mustn't start thinking like that, because she couldn't risk that sort of conversation. And anyway, she could tell from his expression that he wanted to talk about something different. That appealing, embarrassed look in the eyes, the way he was hesitating, screwing up the courage to start. They all meant that he was feeling responsible towards her. Dutiful. And she couldn't *bear* him when he was like that.

Oh well, best to get it over with. Hannah climbed the last few stairs, trying to forget the heavy weight in her bag.

Doug gave an uncertain grin. 'Had a good look round down there?'

So that was it. *Have you been snooping?* Why could no one in this house ever say things directly? Hannah smiled, blankly. 'It's very interesting.'

Doug hovered. Blast it, if he wanted to say something, why couldn't he get on and say it? At this rate, she wouldn't be able to do *anything* before tea.

'Mr Honeyball mentioned that you'd found the French Terror,' Doug said at last, as though he had to squeeze the words out. 'He wanted the key to—'

'Yes, well, he's bound to be interested in it, isn't he?' Hannah said briskly. 'Seeing he's so crazy about Samuel Roscoe.'

She took a step away from him, down the corridor, and he suddenly began to talk at double speed, as though he was afraid she would get away before he had said his piece.

'Look, the French Terror doesn't work. It's dangerous, Hannah and you ought to leave it alone. I can't really explain about it, but you have to believe me, because I know, I really do. Don't start messing about with it.'

Hannah felt the weight in the bag dragging at her arm. 'Lucky you couldn't find the key then, wasn't it?'

His eyes slid away from her and she thought, *He knows. He knows we've got it.* For a second she thought he was going to challenge her and make her admit it, but instead he put a hand gently on her arm.

'Hannah, I know I can't really interfere with what you and Stephen do. Not—not the way things are. But you can't expect me just to stand aside and watch you—'

His voice caught in his throat and Hannah closed her mind. Whatever he was going to say, she didn't want to hear it. Almost without thinking, she looked down at her watch.

And he saw her, of course. She hadn't meant it, she really hadn't consciously meant it as a snub, but he saw it like that. Immediately he dropped his hand and stepped away from her, leaving her way clear, waving her past.

'Sorry. Like I said, I know I shouldn't interfere.'

She felt like shaking him. 'Why do you have to *apologize* all the time? What are you apologizing for?'

She said it louder than she meant to, because she felt guilty, and he was so surprised that he looked her straight in the eye. She thought, she actually thought, that he was going to tell her something for once.

'I—'

'Yes?' She tried not to sound too eager.

But it was no use. His eyes slid away from her face and he smiled that silly smile, spread his hands and shrugged. 'Oh, I don't know. Being here, I suppose. I should have gone away years ago, shouldn't I?'

Grovel, grovel, cringe, cringe. *I don't* want *to pity you. Can't you understand that? I want—I want—* Exasperated, Hannah stepped past him.

'Don't be stupid. If you went away, who would look after Uncle Ernest?'

O.K., so it was the wrong answer, so it wasn't kind. How could any of them be kind to each other, the way things were? If he didn't like it, he ought to do something about it. Or was he afraid he'd bodge that up too, the way he bodged up everything else?

Thoroughly bad-tempered, Hannah stepped out along the gallery.

Chapter 10

Stephen stood outside the library door and looked at his watch. Two minutes to four. It didn't seem very polite to remind Nick that he was supposed to be coming to tea, but Mother would go on about it for ever and ever if he forgot. Stephen knocked and pushed the door open.

'Oh, hallo.' Nick blinked up at him. He was sitting at the desk, making notes. 'Something wrong?'

'No. I just came to see if you were ready. For tea.'

'Ready? What? Oh yes!' Nick jumped up guiltily.

'I think—' Stephen hesitated, but then decided that he ought to say it. 'Have you forgotten your shoes?'

'What?' Nick looked down at his scarlet socks.'Oh, thanks. I always kick them off when I'm sitting at a desk. Hang on.'

He fished them out from under his chair and bent down to tie them up, talking as he did so.

'I know what I meant to ask you. You don't know what happened to that photograph, do you?'

Stephen was glad he wasn't being watched. 'Photograph?'

'Yes, you know. The one of the French Terror. I've found something else about it, that's all, and I thought it might be quite interesting to put them together. You can have a transcript of the letters Samuel Roscoe wrote about it, as well. The whole lot should make a nice little exhibition to put beside the French Terror when you open the Collection.'

'That's a good idea,' Stephen said, hoping the question about the photograph wasn't coming up again. He was lucky. By the time Nick stood up, his mind had moved on.

'It's all coming together, isn't it? How's the back drive?'

97

He sounded quite excited. 'Getting near the Lion Gates yet?'

'I—' Stephen swallowed hard. Until today, opening the collection had seemed something that belonged to the distant future. But now, suddenly, it was all closing in on him. 'I'm almost halfway,' he lied.

'Oh.' Nick looked surprised. Disappointed. 'Well anyway, you might like to see—'

Stephen opened the door, but just before Nick reached it he stopped and bent down to pick something off one of the heaps on the floor. A piece of yellow paper from a bundle of pieces of yellow paper.

'I found this. It's interesting to see that the French Terror—'

Stephen glanced down at his watch. Two minutes past four. 'Actually I think we should go now, or we'll be late.'

'O.K.' Amiably, Nick pushed the piece of paper into his pocket. 'I'll show you in a minute.'

Stephen nodded, but he wasn't really listening. He was gritting his teeth, getting ready to endure the tea party. He knew it was going to be all wrong, had even said it to his mother, as clearly as he dared. ('I don't think Nick will expect anything special.') But nothing would put her off. She had spent the whole morning making thin, triangular sandwiches and little, dry cakes. Worst of all, she had dusted down the big drawing room and taken the dustsheets off the chairs. ('It's not polite to treat visitors casually, Stephen.')

Longingly, Stephen imagined a tea party in the kitchen. Bread and honey and a huge pot of tea. They could have sat around with their feet up and relaxed and Nick would have been jolly and told jokes. But there was no chance that he would relax in the huge drawing room, sitting on one of the stiffly padded chairs. If you even leaned backwards in one of those, it slid across the room on its castors. Sighing, Stephen pushed the door open.

Mrs Roscoe looked even smaller than usual, sitting in a chair by the fireplace, halfway down the room. Stephen wondered whether she had consciously arranged her hands to cover the worn patches on the chair arms. Around her were chairs and trolleys and little tables pulled into a stiff, awkward circle. She had probably meant to make it look cosy, but it wasn't. It looked marooned in the middle of a great sea of carpet.

As Stephen and Nick stepped into the room, she stood up, a moment too early, waiting in a stiff, welcoming pose for them to reach her. Somehow that made the room seem even larger.

'Good afternoon, Mr Honeyball. I'm glad you could spare the time from your work to come and have tea.'

That's not fair, Stephen thought angrily. *We're only four minutes late. What's she fussing about?* Nick seemed not to notice that he was being criticized though.

'It's very good of you to ask me, Mrs Roscoe.' He wandered down the room towards her, looking around as though he hadn't already been shown it. Understandable, really, because it was different with the dustsheets off, but Stephen felt like giving him a push.

'Please sit down,' Mrs Roscoe said. 'There are plenty of chairs.' And she caught Stephen's eye.

'Oh yes, yes of course,' Nick said, when Stephen touched his elbow. He sat down unwisely on the chair next to Mrs Roscoe and slid backwards. 'Sorry. Clumsy of me.'

He was apologetic already and Stephen tried not to look at him as he sat down himself, more cautiously. It was going to be a disaster.

'Hannah's not here?' Nick said brightly, glancing round as though he expected her to jump out of the huge fireplace or crawl from under the grandpiano.

Mrs Roscoe's mouth tightened faintly. 'She'll be here in a moment, I imagine. Milk, Mr Honeyball?'

'Oh—er—yes please.'

The door opened with a crash and Hannah appeared in the doorway, breathless, with her hair neatly brushed and a clean dress on.

'Sorry I'm late,' she said defiantly as she came down the room. 'I had to stop and talk to Doug on my way over.'

Ouch, Stephen thought. Mother didn't say a word, didn't

twitch an eyebrow, but her anger was present, in the air.

'I'm sure he wouldn't have kept you, Hannah, if you'd told him you were expected here for tea.'

Sorry, I can't stay and talk to you, because Mother's waiting for me. Oh, that would have had the right effect, O.K. Stephen imagined it. Doug would have shrunk away, apologized, effaced himself. Probably not spoken to either of them for months.

Hannah flopped down on to a chair. 'I'm starving.'

'I'm sure you've all been working very hard,' Mrs Roscoe said, catching Hannah's eye and glancing at the plate of sandwiches. (*Why do I always have to tell you everything?*)

Hannah picked it up, of course. Got up politely and offered Nick a sandwich. And after that they were into the tea party routine, where it was impossible to say anything, because the cups were too small and the sandwiches and cakes only lasted for one or two bites.

'Is your work going well?' Mrs Roscoe said to Nick. And then, before he could answer, held out her hand for the thin, bone china cup he had drained in a couple of slurps.

'What?' Nick stuttered nervously. 'Oh yes, please. I'm very thirsty. Dusty stuff, this research.' Then he blushed, realizing what he had said. 'Not that I mean—'

The more nervous he got, the faster he ate, and the more often Mrs Roscoe offered him sandwiches, cakes, cups of tea. Stephen tried to intervene, to slow things down, but he only got a glare from his mother for interrupting, and Hannah wasn't any use. She seemed to be ignoring them all.

Not that she could get away with that for ever. People ought to make polite conversation at tea parties, according to Mrs Roscoe, and Hannah was no exception. When she was looking vaguest, she got a question directed at her.

'And how are you getting on with the catalogue, Hannah? Is it nearly ready for Mr Honeyball?'

For a frightful moment, Hannah looked completely blank, and Stephen was terrified that she was going to give the whole thing away. Then she pulled herself together.

'Oh, the *catalogue*. Yes, it's coming along fine, thank you. Just taking a long time because it's complicated.'

Nick sat up straighter, as though he had remembered something. 'I was interested to see it's been opened to the public in the past.'

'Opened to the public?' Mrs Roscoe raised her eyebrows at him.

Nick nodded. 'The collection of automatons. No one told me it had ever been exhibited.'

There was a short, stiff silence. Then Mrs Roscoe said, 'I think you are mistaken.'

'No, I don't think so.' Nick felt in his pockets. 'I was going to show you, Stephen, when we were in the library.'

He pulled out the piece of yellow paper and passed it to Stephen. It was a small handbill, not very well laid out and rather crudely printed.

THE ROSCOE ROBOTS

an exceptional exhibition of
eighteenth and nineteenth century automatons

Open	Mon. – Fri.	10.00 am – 4.00 pm
	Sat. – Sun.	10.00 am – 5.30 pm

Admission	Adults	50p
	Children under 14	25p

'May I see?' Mrs Roscoe reached out and twitched the paper from Stephen's hands while he was still reading it.

'It can't have been very long ago,' Nick said helpfully. 'I'm surprised you don't know about it. Perhaps I'd better ask Mr Roscoe—'

Mrs Roscoe's hand jerked suddenly and hit the cup of tea on the little table beside her, knocking it off on to the carpet. The precious Aubusson carpet. Tea flooded over a patch of pale flowers and the delicate, brittle handle snapped off the cup. One of the Royal Worcester cups.

Nick was on his feet at once. 'Shall I fetch a cloth?'

'Please don't worry. It doesn't matter at all.' Mrs Roscoe

managed to sound almost casual. Stephen wondered whether the others had noticed her fist clench tight round the screwed-up handbill. 'It was very clumsy of me.'

Extraordinarily clumsy. The sort of thing she had never done, as far as Stephen could remember.

'There's not a lot spilt.' Helpfully, Nick took out his handkerchief and began to scrub at the carpet, spreading the tea even further and rubbing the stain into the pile.

'Thank you,' Mrs Roscoe said.

Thank you? Stephen stared at her. There was Nick, ruining the carpet, and Mother was hardly paying attention. Even though she was looking straight at the rubbing handkerchief, her eyes were vague, as though she was too preoccupied with something else to care about furnishings. But that was impossible.

Until the cup went flying, Hannah had managed to cut herself off from the polite party chatter. Not difficult. All you had to do was fix a smile on your face and nod every now and then while you were passing the sandwiches. Then you could keep your brain for important things.

Like weights.

Eight pound weights, to be precise. She had just had time to sneak up to the Egyptian bathroom before tea and drag out the scales that Mother kept hidden in one of the black-and-gold cupboards. With the door locked, she had pulled the brass lump out of her toolbag and weighed it.

And now she had to think of a substitute. Something around the house that could be tied to the cord inside the other pillar. Mentally, while the others chattered, she searched the house, room by room, trying to think what would be heavy and relatively small. Something metal? Something stone?

And then the tea cup went over and there was instant chaos. Nick leaped up to help, looking as upset as though he'd done it himself. Stephen hovered miserably, wanting to stop Nick rubbing and scrubbing, but not knowing how to do it. And Mother—

But no, Mother wasn't fussing. She was sitting watching what was going on and looking somehow—incompetent.

Suddenly Hannah wanted to be out of the way.

'Let's do the washing up,' she said loudly.

That fetched Nick, as she had meant it to. He jumped up from the carpet and began piling cups and plates on to the trolley. Mother frowned and muttered something about visitors, but she didn't actually try to stop them. And that was odd too.

'Do you really think we ought to let Nick help?' Stephen hissed in Hannah's ear as they followed the trolley up the room. 'Suppose he breaks something?'

'Then he'll probably burst into tears,' muttered Hannah briskly. She broke into a trot to catch up with Nick as he reached the door. The trolley was difficult to steer and he looked all set to ram the door frame.

'Through there, isn't it?' Nick jerked his head at the service door across the hall. 'And then the third door along the corridor. Yes?'

'The second, actually.' Hannah grabbed the trolley and gave it a bit of unobtrusive guidance. 'We use the old butler's pantry for our kitchen. The main kitchen's much too big for us.'

Nick drooped slightly. 'Do you think your mother would mind if I just—I haven't liked to look at that part of the house in case I disturbed her, but it would be nice to see—'

'No problem.' Hannah shoved the trolley into the service corridor and ditched it. 'You get started, Stephen. I'll show off the sights.'

She marched past the pantry and flung open the kitchen door, stepping aside to let Nick have a good view. He stood in the doorway for a second and then walked slowly in.

Hannah grinned. 'Good, isn't it? Much better than all that classy stuff in the drawing room.'

'Gadgets,' Nick said with relish. 'Tools. They're what old Sam really liked, you see. He must be the only millionaire who ever furnished his own kitchen, down to the last potato peeler.'

That made sense. The oil paintings in the drawing room looked as if they'd been bought by the square yard, but the kitchen was different. Every high-tech-gadget-of-a-hundred-years-ago that money could buy was there, from the Stevenson Variable Chopping Machine to the Patent Marmalade Mill. Knife cleaners and coffee grinders, egg coddlers and cream beaters. And even a hand-operated washing machine out in the laundry room.

And then there were the tools. Copper pans ranged in rows and fancy moulds that filled the cupboards to bursting. Sieves and knives and brushes and shakers and spoons and forks. And, brooding over everything, at the far end of the room, the huge black kitchen range with its dozens of little handles and lids and doors.

It was all just too perfect, though. Fossilized like an exhibition. Everything shone too brightly or was scrubbed too clean. And everything was placed too precisely in exactly the right place, from the vast cast-iron ham kettle to the last little brass weight gleaming beside the scales.

The last little—

I'm dumb, Hannah thought. *I'm as thick as pea soup.* There she was, racking her brains to think of a weight she could use, when the kitchen was full of weights.

Leaving Nick to experiment with the sugar cutter, she wandered over to the big dresser and looked greedily at the weights. Quarter ounce, half ounce, ounce . . . The little ones were brass discs, stacked in a neat pyramid. But the bigger ones were black cast iron cubes, with a bar set into the top to act as a handle. Ideal for tying to a piece of cord. The eight pound one was the largest, standing massively at the end of the perfectly-spaced line.

Hannah gripped the handle and lifted it down, swinging her arm slightly to feel how it moved. Yes. Not bad. It was a different shape from the brass cylinder that should have been in the French Terror, but it would be a fair substitute. If she could have it. The only problem was that it left a noticeable gap on the shelf. She narrowed her eyes, considering. Perhaps if she moved all the others along an inch or two . . .

'Mind if I look in the cupboards?' Nick said, from the other side of the room.

Hannah nodded, without thinking, and the next moment

there was a deafening clatter that went on and on. He had opened the cupboard full of cake tins and the precarious pile inside had toppled over. Round ones and square ones of every size. Swiss-roll tins, patty tins, ring moulds and brioche moulds and the big wooden icing mould that balanced at the back. They went sliding and rolling all over the floor and Nick stood watching them, with his mouth open, looking appalled.

'Idiot,' Hannah said. She strolled across the kitchen still swinging the weight. 'It'll take us about a hundred years to pick them all up.'

'I hope none of them are damaged—'

'Probably all dented past repair,' Hannah said cheerfully. 'Don't break your heart. No one will ever use them again.'

'What's going on?' Stephen appeared suddenly in the doorway. He sounded quite calm, but he must have sprinted down the corridor. 'You haven't broken—?'

Nick looked distressed. 'I really wasn't doing anything—'

'Listen, they're fine.' Hannah stopped teasing him and picked up the icing mould in her free hand. 'You don't suppose Samuel Roscoe let his cook buy rubbish, do you? Now let's pick them up. If we hurry, we can get them back in the cupboard before Mother appears.'

Stephen grabbed up an armful while she was still speaking and stacked them tidily together. As he turned round from putting them in the cupboard, he glanced across at the dresser, noticing the gap. 'What's happened to the—?'

Hannah swung her arm forward to let him see the weight. 'It's here.'

That had the two of them baffled, all right. She let them goggle for a moment while she looked smug and then she broke it to them casually.

'If I use this, I can get the French Terror working.'

Good thing she wasn't expecting applause. Nick seemed quite pleased, but Stephen looked as if she had dropped the weight on his foot. Just for a minute. Then he put on his irritating goody-goody expression.

'Mother will never say yes.'

'So who's asking her? I'll just smuggle it out of the kitchen when she's not around.'

'But you can't—'

Hannah felt like braining him with the weight. There she was, about to restore an old, valuable piece of clockwork, and he was behaving as if she was stealing sultanas. What did it matter if she borrowed the weight? She was hardly going to damage a lump of cast iron.

But before she could point that out, Mrs Roscoe put her head round the door. Looked at Nick and the tumbled tins, and then at Hannah and the weight.

'Ah,' she said.

'I'm sorry.' Nick waved an arm. 'I had a slight accident when I opened the cupboard. But I'll pick them all up.'

'No, that's all right. I'll do them.' Mrs Roscoe knelt down, quite unnecessarily, and began to pick up the cake tins and dust them down, as though they had fallen into a rubbish heap instead of on to a spotless floor.

Hannah edged backwards nearer to the dresser. If she could slip the weight into its place on the shelf, Mother might forget that she had been carrying it. Then she could sneak back and borrow it later on. She was just raising her hand to put it next to the four pound weight, when Mrs Roscoe glanced up at her.

'That's rather a strange thing to be showing Mr Honeyball, isn't it?'

Hannah swung the weight again. 'I just wanted him to see how heavy—'

'Actually,' Stephen interrupted, red in the face, 'we wanted to borrow it. If that's all right.'

Hannah turned round and stared at him. Was he crazy?

There was a small, icy pause. '*Borrow* it?' Mrs Roscoe said. She glanced from Stephen to Hannah and then across at Nick and her whole body was tense and still. *As if she knows why we want it.*

But that was impossible. Nobody could be that good at guessing. And Hannah didn't intend to start believing in telepathy.

'But Stephen,' Mrs Roscoe sounded gently amazed when

she spoke at last. 'That weight is part of a set and these things are valuable. Anyway, what could you possibly need it for?'

'We—' Stephen stammered and stopped.

'We won't do it any harm,' Hannah said stubbornly. 'How could we?'

She swung the weight once more, fiercely, expertly missing a shelf full of blue and white tureens by a mere half an inch. Mrs Roscoe flinched backwards suddenly, over-reacting to the violence. *Good!* Hannah thought, with a kind of savage pleasure. *I wish I could smash the lot.*

But she didn't, of course. And, in another second, Mrs Roscoe had pulled herself together. She walked across the kitchen, took the weight from Hannah's hand and put it back on the dresser. Straightened it, stepped back to look and then straightened it again.

'There. That's better.'

Hannah dug her fingernails into the palms of her hands and glowered at Stephen's back. No chance of sneaking the weight away now. Mother would make a point of keeping an eye on it.

Mrs Roscoe turned back to the tumbled cake tins. 'Don't worry about these, now. It's tricky getting them all into the cupboard. You don't want to waste your time on things like that.'

Nick looked appropriately miserable.

'What about the washing up?' Mrs Roscoe added. 'Have you finished it, or shall I—?'

In other words, get on with it, you lazy slobs, thought Hannah. Stephen took the excuse, of course. He leapt down the corridor like a terrified rabbit, but Hannah wasn't going to let him get away with that. She stormed after him into the butler's pantry and slammed the door after her.

'And what was all *that* about?'

'All what?' Stephen picked up the dishmop and turned his back on her, but she grabbed it out of his hand.

'You know what I mean. If you hadn't *asked* about that weight, I could have come back later and got it. Now that's impossible. And you knew just as well as I did that she would say no. Didn't you?'

He stood silent, looking down at the ground.

'What's the matter?' Hannah scowled at him. 'Don't you want me to mend the French Terror? Don't you want us to open the Collection?'

'You didn't have to have that weight,' Stephen muttered. 'You can always find something else.'

'Correction,' Hannah said sharply. '*You* can find something else. Now. I want an eight pound weight that will fit inside one of those hollow pillars. And don't come back until you've got one!'

She wrenched the door open—and there was Nick standing outside, trying not to listen and waiting to do the washing up. Angrily, Hannah planted the palm of her hand between Stephen's shoulder blades.

'Go on. Hunt. You've got half an hour.'

She shoved him up the corridor and watched him start to climb the back stairs, and then she turned back to Nick. But he had gone into the pantry and was quietly drying up the tea plates. Suddenly, Hannah felt horribly embarrassed.

Chapter 11

Stephen went slowly up the back stairs with his own voice ringing in his ears. *Actually we wanted to borrow it . . . borrow it . . . borrow it . . .*

His mind wriggled, making excuses. It wasn't their weight. You shouldn't take things without asking. How could he have guessed what Mother would say?

Kid's stuff.

It was no use against the words that moved in the darkness of his head, to the echo of Uncle Ernest's laughter. *She wouldn't give up the weight . . . She'll be guilty for ever . . . She wouldn't give up the weight . . .*

That had nothing to do with it. Why should it have anything to do with it? He dragged on up the stairs, feeling groggy and befuddled, as though someone had knocked him over the head. Up and up and up, until he found himself on the top stair, looking along the attic corridor.

Oh well, that was as good a place as any to start looking for Hannah's weight. That's what he was doing. Sensibly. Rationally. He was going to the back attic to find an eight pound weight to take down to Hannah.

He kept telling himself that, while his feet took him automatically along the narrow corridor, past cramped bedrooms where brass bedsteads stood waiting for servants who never came. Along to the very last boxroom at the end, moving with senseless, irrational determination.

He pushed the door open and stepped quietly inside.

No mess, of course. Mother wasn't one to keep the main rooms tidy and tumble things higgledy-piggledy into corners. There was the same order and control everywhere. Everything she had stored away was neatly packed up. The cast-off clothes, the old shoes, the worn-out sheets and the faded curtains. Spare rickety cupboards stood in line with broken chairs and hipbaths. Everything small was in boxes and bags, with space left between the piles so that nothing was out of reach.

Yes, this was the sensible place to start looking. There was bound to be something here that would do for Hannah, otherwise why had he come? He stood in the doorway looking round and then, with hands that felt heavier than any weight, he began to sort through the box nearest to him.

An old, broken hairdryer that someone had tried—and failed—to stick together.

A pack of playing cards. Bent.

A silk scarf printed with a regimental badge.

At the silk scarf, he suddenly caught his breath, so hard that he thought he was going to choke. The feel of it between his fingers. And his mother's voice. Brisk. Cold.

That's right, Stephen. Let's leave them up here until you're bigger. They're not really very safe, are they?

They—

His fingers reached under the scarf for the next thing. Felt knotted string and wooden corners. When he pulled the bundle out, his hands were trembling.

It was an orange string bag, full of bits of wood. He began to pull the pieces out, one by one, and as each piece came out, his mind said, *Yes, yes.*

A big Noah's Ark with a loose, badly-fitting roof. It wobbled when he stood it on the floor and he was ready to bet that it would sink if he tried to sail it.

Two strange, misshapen wooden elephants.

A couple of monkeys, a pair of peacocks and a lion and a lioness, all hacked out of soft, rather grubby wood.

The Noah family, all different sizes, and half a dozen indeterminate shapes that could have been cats or dogs or almost anything with four legs and a tail. And—*yes, yes*—the two swans with their curved necks cut foolishly across the grain of the wood. They had both snapped off, leaving raw, jagged ends.

The moment Stephen saw them, he wondered how he

could have forgotten. Every knife-cut, every sloppily painted brush-stroke could have been Doug's signature. They were unmistakably his handiwork. And he had held them so proudly when he walked across the gallery with them. Stephen could see it in his mind now, precise and distant.

Guess what I've made you, Stephen.

He had stopped halfway and held the string bag out in both hands, with an excited, shame-faced smile, while Stephen ran towards him. Down a longer, higher gallery towards a larger, taller Doug.

The shape of the wooden boat inside the string bag had been magical. *You wanted to take the animals out and play with them. Remember?* Stephen remembered grabbing the bag and turning to show his mother.

'Look! Look what I've got!'

But, as he turned, the lid flew off the Ark and the animals spilled out on to the polished parquet floor. Elephants, monkeys, peacocks, little men and women—and two swans whose brittle necks snapped as they hit the ground at his mother's feet.

She looked down at them.

Not a word. But, even at four, he had been able to read the expression on her face. *More of Doug's rubbish.* A look that shrank the lions and turned the peacocks' jewelled tails to badly-shaped bits of wood, crudely smeared with paint. Slowly he bent down and started to pick the animals up, hiding his face so that Doug wouldn't guess how his present had been ruined.

Even then, it might not have been too bad. But as he picked up the string bag and spread open the top so that he could put the animals back in, his mother had noticed it for the first time.

'That bag? You used *that* bag?'

He could hear, in his mind, the exact tone of her voice, even now. Not loud, but violent, shocked. And he could feel how her hand had gripped his shoulder, hustling him away while she began persuading him to let go of the bag of animals.

He could understand why she had disliked the little animals. Nothing Doug made could ever have been good enough for her ideas of perfection. But what was so wrong with the *bag*? He stood the animals in a row beside the Ark and spread the bag out in front of them.

It was just a grubby orange string bag, with worn leather handles. A shopping bag. At some time or other it had split across the bottom and had been lashed roughly together with more string. Frayed green string. No prizes for guessing who had done that. It was sloppy, but not shocking.

So why had his mother reacted like that? Harshly enough to drag him away, harshly enough to make him give up the toys that had been made for him because he liked the Noah's Ark automaton. He hadn't given them up easily, either. He could remember shouting and crying as she took them away from him.

Stephen sat on the wooden floor of the attic, cradling the peacocks in one hand and looking down at the string bag. He had forgotten that he was supposed to be looking for a weight for Hannah. All he could remember was the feel of his mother's fingers, sliding under his and unhooking them from the bag. And the sound of his own voice, screaming.

'But I want them, I want them! Daddy made them! Daddy made them specially for me!'

Nick spread the damp teatowel over the edge of the wooden draining-board as carefully as Mrs Roscoe herself would have done. Hannah found that she was almost holding her breath waiting for him to turn round. Ridiculous. What did it matter what he thought of her? If she wanted to shout at her own brother, she would shout as loudly as she liked. She was annoyed to find that she was still holding her breath and waiting for Nick to turn.

But he spoke first. 'Fancy coming out and having a hack at the rhododendrons?'

'What?' It was so far from what she had expected him to say that she couldn't think of an answer.

'I think Stephen could do with a hand,' Nick said. 'Before tea, he told me that he wasn't halfway down the drive yet. That's not very good. And since he's gone to look for your weight . . .'

'Oh, I suppose so,' said Hannah grumpily.

'I'll come too.' Nick turned round at last, looking mischievous. 'Hacking at something will do your feelings a world of good.'

Hannah stamped off into the entrance hall, not amused. Her feelings were her own concern. Nothing to do with him. She had reached the stairs before he caught her up, but neither of them spoke until they were in the middle of the gallery. Then Nick glanced sideways, peering through the glass at the broken bridge over the waterfall.

'It's a pity about that. The view from up there is so tremendous that it would be nice to have it mended.'

'I expect we will when we've got some money,' Hannah said grimly. She still hadn't forgiven him. 'Not that we'll ever do that, unless Stephen stops fooling about.'

Nick stood still, slowly running a finger up the arching metal rib that ran between the two panes of glass. 'You're not—' He hesitated and stopped.

'Why do you do that?' Hannah was actually bad tempered enough to say it out loud. 'If you want to say something, then *say* it!'

'All right then.' Nick rubbed his finger harder against the metal. 'I was just going to say that—well—things are pretty straightforward for you, aren't they?'

'*Straightforward?*' Hannah growled. 'With a mother who's incapable of saying what she means, and a brother who's taken to behaving like a lunatic, and a father—'

She hesitated herself this time, but she was caught in her own trap. Nick just glanced at her. *All right*, she thought defiantly, *I will say it*.

'—a father who lives on the other side of the stream.'

Nick went pink. 'Actually, I thought he must be—'

'O.K., so you guessed.' Hannah managed a short, sharp laugh. 'It's not a *secret*. We just don't go on about it.'

'That's all?' Nick said. 'File it away and get on with something else?'

'That's all,' said Hannah firmly. Why shouldn't it be? Things had been like that for—what?—eight years or so. She'd just come home from school at the end of the summer term and found Doug living on the other side of the house. No explanations, except a quick sentence from Mother. *It's better like this for a bit*, said with the kind of frown that stopped you asking any more questions. And ever since then, it had been the same. Doug on one side, looking after Uncle Ernest, and the rest of them on the other, looking after the house. And Doug and Mother never meeting, never speaking. Hannah scowled at Nick. 'Anyway, it's none of your business, is it?'

She thought that would shut him up for the rest of the afternoon, but it didn't. He looked red and hot and uncomfortable, but he answered her.

'I'm not prying into that. What I wanted to say was about Stephen.'

'Hmmph.' Hannah looked uninviting, but Nick ploughed on.

'I don't think he's as good as you are at filing things away when they bother him.'

'What's *that* supposed to mean?' Hannah glared. This was turning into the sort of conversation she particularly hated, about people's feelings. 'What's wrong with Stephen?

Nick frowned. 'I don't know. But he's not happy about having the French Terror mended, is he? And he certainly doesn't want to believe that it's been mended before.'

'Because of that photograph?' Hannah pulled a face. 'Well, that could have been faked, couldn't it?'

'Not just the photograph.' Nick shook his head. 'He didn't look very pleased about the handbill, either, and nor did your mother.'

'Handbill?' Hannah looked vague. Nick obviously expected her to know what he was talking about, but she didn't recall seeing the crumpled piece of yellow paper that he pushed at her. She smoothed it out and read it.

114

```
┌─────────────────────────────────────────────────┐
│              THE ROSCOE ROBOTS                    │
│                                                   │
│              an exceptional exhibition of         │
│        eighteenth and nineteenth century automatons│
│                                                   │
│   Open   Mon. – Fri.      10.00 am – 4.00 pm      │
│          Sat. – Sun.      10.00 am – 5.30 pm      │
│                                                   │
│          Admission   Adults        50p            │
│          Children under 14         25p            │
│                                                   │
│          See the soldiers march!!!                │
│          Watch the animals play!!!!               │
│   Shudder at the horrors of the French Terror!!!!!│
│                                                   │
└─────────────────────────────────────────────────┘
```

Nick peered over her arm. 'It must have worked then.'

'But it could have been years ago.'

'Not that long. Look at the prices. And the style of printing. It must have been within the last twenty years, and I'm ready to bet it was between five and ten years ago.'

'But that's silly.' Hannah frowned. 'I would remember if it was that recently.'

Nick looked uncomfortable. 'You might have been— away at school.'

Oh no, Hannah thought angrily. Not back to that again. 'Well, Stephen would have been here. He would remember.'

Nick didn't answer. He just went on rubbing away at the arched metal rib with the tip of one finger.

'But that's ridiculous!' Hannah burst out. 'You mean he does remember and he's hiding it from us?'

'You *are* straightforward, aren't you?' Nick grinned, unexpectedly. 'No, I didn't mean that. But I think— perhaps—he might be hiding it from himself. Because he doesn't want to remember.'

For a moment, Hannah struggled to imagine what it would be like trying not to remember something when you couldn't remember what it was that you were trying not to remember . . .

'That doesn't make sense,' she said at last.

'It doesn't have to make sense,' Nick said gently. 'It's just something that happens sometimes. I don't know, of course. But several times I've had a feeling about him . . . something I couldn't quite pin down . . . I'm not happy about what we're doing, Hannah.'

'What do you *mean*?' Hannah felt frustrated. How could you talk about something that wasn't quite anything? 'Would it be better if we talked to him? Tried to get him to remember?'

'No, of course not!' Nick almost snapped the words. 'You can't take people to pieces like clockwork, just because you want to know what goes on inside them. I mean—perhaps we ought to leave it alone.'

Hannah felt like grabbing his hand and bashing it through the glass. This was the *most* stupid conversation she had ever had. 'Why did you start talking about it then?'

He swallowed. She saw his adam's apple bob up and down, ridiculously knobbly in his thin neck. 'I mean *really* leave it alone. Stop this whole business.'

'*Stop mending the French Terror*?'

Nick looked miserable. 'No, worse than that. Stop the whole idea of opening the Collection. It seems to be stirring up things—'

'But it was *your* idea. You wanted it more than anyone did.' *We can't stop now. We can't.* Hannah was so angry that she couldn't bear to go on talking to him. She ran to the end of the gallery and tugged at the frayed bellstring, flinging it to the ground when it came off in her hand. Why did Doug have to keep the door shut anyway?

When he opened it, she could hardly bring herself not to snarl at him. She just managed a quick, tight smile. 'O.K. if I come through?'

She was in before he gave her an answer, running along the corridor and down the stairs. But as soon as she got near the billiard room, she knew that it was no use touching the French Terror. She hadn't got either of the weights, and her hands were shaking with rage. It would be disastrous to go anywhere near a piece of machinery. Blow Nick!

116

He was right about one thing, though. What she needed was a chance to hack and chop and bash at something. She pushed open the gun room door, grabbed the shears from under the dull eyes of the stuffed pheasants and let herself out of the back door. Upstairs she could hear Nick saying polite things to Doug. Good. She hoped they kept at it all the rest of the afternoon.

From what Nick had said, she expected to find a tangle of bushes when she had gone a few yards down the drive. But the way was clear as far as she could see, at least until the drive bent. Shouldering the shears, she marched forward, her other fist clenched, her teeth gritted, her face set into an angry scowl.

But it was very quiet on the path under the trees, still and cool and silent. Somehow, as she walked, her anger evaporated. What was she getting so worked up about anyway? Why did it matter if Nick was nosy? She would probably have been the same in his place. They were a peculiar family, after all. Working with the Collection had made her too touchy. She had been shut up alone, with the glass eyes and the jewelled eyes and the painted eyes all staring at her.

When she heard Nick coming up behind, she loitered and let him catch up with her and they walked on along the drive together. And on and on and on.

It was almost a quarter of a mile before they stopped. Their way was blocked by a few brambles and a thick undergrowth of roadside weeds, but there was nothing tall enough to block their view of the Lion gateway. The gateway that led out on to the road.

The lions were small and neat, carved out of honey-coloured stone. Once they had stood upright on their pillars, each holding a shield between his front feet. But for years the right hand pillar had been slewed sideways, leaning against a large tree. And the left hand lion had met with an accident last summer. The pillar was knocked over and the broken lion's head had rolled a few feet backwards into the rhododendrons.

Bending down, Nick reached under a couple of branches and touched it, as if he couldn't really believe that he was so close to the end of the drive. Then he looked round at Hannah.

'Almost halfway. That's what Stephen said to me at teatime. I thought he was being pessimistic, but—'

No need to finish the sentence, Hannah thought grimly. She stared at the fallen pillar. *Cracked. Just like*—For a moment, Stephen's pale, tense face swam into her mind, but she pushed the picture away. No, she wouldn't think like that. Stephen was all *right*.

Chapter 12

The string wound itself into patterns in Stephen's brain as he stared at it. Orange and green, snaking across his eyes, knotting itself into his retina in sharp angles, moving, moving, always moving so that he could never find the beginning of the pattern. Like a spider's web with no centre, like a maze with no middle.

The key had let them in to find the French Terror, and the photograph and the handbill showed that it could be made to work, and the weight would get it going. But where did the string bag belong? It wasn't eighteenth century, it had nothing to do with the French Terror, it was irrelevant. It *had* to be irrelevant.

But the dark figures began to move in the back of his mind, stepping jerkily like the monsters in midnight horror films. And then something dark that moved fast, *fast*—

DANGER!

His brain screamed it at him. Went into a spasm, incapable of thinking. Incapable of working anything out reasonably.

DANGER!

DANGER!

And then, suddenly—nothing.

It was as if the whole world had gone away. Everything was still and quiet and he was alone in the attic, staring down at the crumpled bag and the heap of wooden animals. No noise in his head. Just a single, simple idea.

Get rid of the French Terror.

He blinked and the polite, careful Stephen in the front of his mind looked at the idea and tossed it away. Ridiculous.

Get rid of the French Terror.

119

Tidily, he began to push the wooden animals back into the bag. Every one, even the broken swans and the little, lumpy hen. He was perfectly all right, except that for some reason he was finding it a little difficult to breathe. Perfectly calm and reasonable and not at all in danger of doing anything stupid.

Get rid of the French Terror.

What he ought to do was go to his bedroom and get out his Physics project. It wasn't long till the beginning of next term and he hadn't even looked at it yet. Old Hansen would go spare. Yes, he would go to his bedroom.

Standing up, he tottered slightly. There was a stiffness in his knees as though he had knelt for longer than he realized. He walked awkwardly to the stairs and began to go down, stopping every now and again to catch his breath. It was absurd, the way he couldn't breathe properly. Stop, breathe and on again.

It was only when he reached the very bottom of the stairs that he realized he wasn't going to his bedroom. His feet had taken him way down, below his bedroom, below the kitchens, to the cellars in the rock.

The part of his brain that he could contact noticed the cold dampness of the air on his skin as he went through to the back cellar. The feel of the ribbed plastic under his fingers as he picked up the flashlight. The dust on the raised letters on the front of the furnace, shadowy in the flashlight beam.

The three paraffin cans standing in a row against the wall.

But that part of his brain was only an observer, not connected to the rest of his body. It had not ordered his legs to walk across to the paraffin cans. Had not told his right hand to reach out and pick them up, one after the other, testing the weights to see which was the fullest.

His fingers closed round the handle of the fullest can and he began to move back towards the door. Then stopped. Slowly, his eyes scanned the cellar. A heap of coke. Old boxes of newspaper. A basket with a broken handle, full of kindling wood. Yes.

Putting down everything except the flashlight, he tipped the kindling out into a heap, tidying up the bits that fell to one side and putting them with the others.

When he turned to pick up the paraffin can, he was surprised to see the string bag full of animals lying beside it. For a moment he was thrown, as though the thing had eerily pursued him by itself. Then he realized that he must have kept hold of it. Must have carried it all the way down from the attic. But it had nothing to do with—

Get rid of the French Terror.

Thought blanked out again. He was watching himself, like someone watching a film. He saw himself lift the paraffin can into the basket, jam in the bag of animals beside it, and then take a newspaper from the box to cover the top. He tucked the edges in carefully, so that nothing could be seen. Every movement was steady and perfectly normal. His mind was cold and clear and detached. Everything was quite ordinary.

Except that he still couldn't breathe properly. And somewhere, deep inside his head, he was terrified.

He stood up and walked over to the furnace. Somewhere, just up here, there ought to be . . . Ah yes! His fingers reached the back of the shelf and closed round the big box of matches. That went into the basket too, tucked securely under the newspaper.

Then he was on his way, walking steadily up the back stairs. Out through the servants' door and into the entrance hall. Art and Industry, Manufactures and Commerce, clutched their brushes and pens and machinery like weapons pointed at his head. They stared. Even the heavy patterns on the wallpaper seemed to be staring at him.

'Stephen?'

His ear caught the sound of his mother's voice, judging distance and direction. Drawing room? Library? No, she was doing something in the dining room. That meant he could get to the far end of the gallery before she reached him. She would never follow there. It would mean trouble afterwards, but afterwards was as remote as the Himalayas.

121

He walked steadily out over the stream. Vaguely noticing that the string was missing from the bell, he banged on the door with his hand.

'Hallo?' Now it was Doug's eyes. On him, on the basket. 'The others came through a long time ago. They've gone down the back drive, I think. I wondered where you were.'

No problem. It was easy to answer. Stephen could even look him straight in the eye.

'I was helping Mother clear up the tea. There was a lot left over. She's sent it so that Hannah and I can have a picnic with Nick.'

Doug didn't believe that, of course. Mother would never waste any food that could be saved for tomorrow. And even if she had, she would never send it out to a picnic in a dirty old basket with a piece of newspaper over the top.

It was all nonsense, but that didn't matter. Doug would never challenge him, whatever he said. Because of course he was going to get through. He was going to the French Terror.

Doug leaned forward slightly, towards the basket, trying to peer in. But all he said, half-smiling, half-sad, was, 'Alison's scones?'

Scones by the fire, dripping with butter. Doug grinning and jamming his scone in whole. And Mother, with butter running down her chin, shaking her head and laughing . . . laughing . . . laughing . . .

Stephen remembered it, and he saw Doug looking into his eyes, knowing that he remembered. But it was nothing. It was too late. He waited just a second and then made his voice and his face perfectly blank.

'She never makes scones.'

It ought to have been enough. Stephen expected Doug to shut off at once and let him through. But he didn't. Instead, he reached out and put a hand on Stephen's shoulder.

'I don't want to interfere, but are you sure you're all right?'

It was an intrusion, something he never did, outside the rules. Stephen stood up straighter. Over Doug's shoulder, he could see his own face, pale and pinched, in the spotted mirror on the wall.

'I'm perfectly all right, thank you.'

But the fingers gripped his shoulder firmly, and Doug frowned. 'Stephen—'

He's going to do something, thought Stephen. As if he was seeing pictures, he imagined Doug ripping the basket out of his hand, putting an arm round him. Taking charge. And down at the very bottom of his mind he wished—

'Stephen—'

And then it was over. Doug didn't go on. He stopped, let go of Stephen and drew back, as though something had got in the way at the last moment, preventing him from what he wanted to do. Stephen walked towards the stairs, not hurrying, but stiff and straight-backed, and Doug didn't follow him.

The billiard room was empty, as he had known it would be. Because everything had been meant to be like this from the beginning, from before he was born. He had always been going to come like this, carrying these things, to do what he was going to do. The actions needed no effort. He moved up the room as though he were one of the automatons, fated to do what he did by the arrangement of his cogs, by the shape of his cams.

He stopped in front of the French Terror, put his basket down and pulled off the newspaper. For a second he was baffled by the string bag full of animals. Then he took it out and laid it on the stage, in front of the guillotine.

Now the paraffin. Picking up the can, he unscrewed the top and began to walk slowly round the French Terror, pouring a thin, inflammable trail on to the stage.

'There!' said Hannah. She put down the shears and looked along the drive with satisfaction. 'Clear from the house to the Lion Gates.'

Nick grinned at her expression. 'You like doing that, don't you? Sorting things out. Getting them working again.'

'It's my thing,' Hannah said. 'Like yours is fiddling around with old bills and bits of paper.'

'I'm not just fiddling.' Nick looked injured. 'I'm doing my own kind of sorting out. Attempting to make sense of what happened before we came along. To see the pattern.'

Hannah nodded. That sounded almost like dealing with machinery. 'History repeating itself, you mean.'

'History *not* repeating itself is the exciting thing.' Nick seemed to light up as he spoke. 'Things carry on the same for years and years and then, suddenly, someone steps out of the pattern. Those are the real heroes. People like your great-great-grandfather.'

Old Sam Roscoe with his beard and his drains? 'What's heroic about *him*?' Hannah said scornfully.

Nick stared. 'Well, it's easier and safer to stick with what you know, isn't it? Even if it means being a poor, illiterate stonemason's son. Takes a lot of nerve to risk going off to strange places and dealing with people who look down their noses at you.' He waved a hand backwards, towards the house. 'Samuel Roscoe was pretty brave. Pretty tough. You can feel it in every room of the house. Every inch of this place.'

His face! Like someone talking about Eldorado. And all because of a grumpy old man with a beard. Hannah felt like shuddering, but she nodded instead.

'Well, now the drive's clear, we'll be able to do something about preserving this tough old house. If we get a good number of tourists up this drive, his ghost can go on lurking in Roscoe's Leap.'

She looked him straight in the eye as she said it. *O.K. Mr Clever Nicholas Honeyball, have another go at me if you want to. I've got the answer this time.* She'd worked it out while she was hacking through a tough tangle of briars.

He didn't have a go at her, of course. There was no point in saying the same things all over again. He just raised one eyebrow and waited, so she let him have the explanation anyway.

'I *can't* stop in the middle. Imagine if it was you. If I came along to the library now and said "Right, that's it. You've got to stop working on those silly old papers, even if you haven't finished." Wouldn't you argue?'

'But that's not—'

'Oh yes it is the same. You'd go berserk, wouldn't you? You've got to sort them out, because you've got to know about Samuel Roscoe. And I'm the same about the French Terror. I've sorted out in my mind how it works, but I don't know I'm right. Not for sure. Not until I see it going.'

Nick didn't look quite as flattened as she had expected by her little speech. For a second or two he went on staring at her as if he might be going to argue back. He obviously changed his mind, but he was still solemn when he answered. 'It won't make any difference whatever I say, will it? It's not that I don't understand, but—' He kicked at the heap of branches beside the path. 'Oh never mind. Just be careful, that's all. Be gentle.'

What did he think was going to happen? Did he think she and Stephen were going to fight like a couple of little kids. Hannah felt like braining Nick with the shears, but instead she grinned at him.

'Come with me then, and see if Stephen's found another weight. Then you can hold me down if I'm tempted to bash him.'

She meant, *O.K. I'm not an idiot. I'll go easy on him.* And Nick got the message, even if he wasn't as practised in not-saying things as the Roscoes were. He dropped the anxious look and talked to her about the automatons as they walked back up the drive.

They smelt the paraffin as soon as they stepped inside the house. Nick sniffed and stopped in the middle of a sentence. 'Someone had an accident with a heater?'

As he spoke, there was a noise from the billiard room, as if they had startled someone who had bumped into something. *Doug!* Hannah thought, with a sudden jolt made up of worry and annoyance. If he had seen that the back panel of the French Terror was only propped in place and not screwed on . . .

But it wasn't Doug. It was Stephen, standing up at the far end of the room with the blue paraffin can in one hand and its cap in the other, and the smell of paraffin was coming from the French Terror. Hannah could see it lying on the polished surface of the stage. And the stage sloped backwards to the doors, and behind the doors were the figures in their genuine, eighteenth century, very-inflammable clothes . . .

She took in all that in a single glance and, almost before she had time to make sense of what she had seen she was charging up the room. 'What the bloody hell do you think you're doing?'

Stephen didn't answer. Just blinked stupidly at her and then looked down at the paraffin can.

Hannah waved the shears at him. 'If that stuff catches fire—'

'I'm afraid that's probably the point.' Fingers closed round her hand and Nick gently broke her grip on the shears and took them away. 'The paraffin's all round the stage. Things like that don't happen by accident.'

'Don't be *silly*.' Hannah stepped nearer to Stephen, peering into his face. 'Were you playing some kind of crazy game?'

'He may not be able to—' Nick began.

And, at the same moment, Stephen said, 'I don't know.' Blankly at first and then again, more desperately. 'I don't *know*.'

He put down the paraffin can and stared at his hands like a zombie, as if they had sprinkled paraffin everywhere without telling him. Hannah grabbed the can and the top and screwed the top firmly back on. Then she went to the window seat where her tools were hidden and got a piece of old rag to mop up the paraffin on the stage. There was going to be a scene. She could feel it coming. And she didn't want to be involved.

'Hannah.' Nick gripped her shoulder and pulled her to her feet. 'You can't just turn your back on this and pretend it's not serious.'

She glared at the floor, purposely avoiding his face and Stephen's. 'I know what's going on. It's childish. Stephen's been trying to stop me mending the French Terror all along. He didn't give me the key. Then he was peculiar about the photograph. Then he made sure I couldn't have the weight from the kitchen.' She kicked sulkily at the side of the stage. 'Now he's burning it, just to be on the safe side.'

She heard Nick catch his breath, as if he was working hard to to control his voice. 'Hannah—that's not *childish*.'

'Yes it is. He's just trying to get his own way.'

Go on, she was thinking. *Put on your soft, considerate voice. Try and make out it's not Stephen's fault and I ought to be kind to him.* She was ready to scream at him if he started. Something in her was so shocked and angry that she wanted to lash out, and Nick was a good, soft target.

Which made it a double shock when he spoke again and his voice was sharp and scornful. 'I thought you liked knowing how things work. Or are you too scared to think about *people?*'

She looked up then, all right. And she saw Stephen look up too, as if he had been shaken out of his terrifying calm. Nick's face was fierce.

'Studying machines is the soft option, Hannah. *They* don't force you to take a look at yourself.'

She spat the challenge back at him, not giving in. 'O.K., then, if you're so clever, you tell me how this little lot works. Why is Stephen trying to stop me mending the French Terror? Why is he trying to set fire to it? If it's not childish, it's mad. Is that what you're telling me? That my brother's mad?'

Stephen's eyes flickered, as if the question was already in his head, waiting for an answer.

'Mad? What's that? Just a word,' Nick said. 'If you want to know what Stephen's doing, why don't you ask him?'

Hannah glared. It was all right for Nick. It was easy for him to be smug when it wasn't his family. 'O.K. Let him tell me—'

'No.' Nick shook his head and stepped away, out of her line of vision. 'Ask *him*.'

That left her looking straight at Stephen, with nowhere else to look. She saw what Nick was up to. He was daring

127

her to stop just pretending to be tough and outspoken. Daring her to ask a real person a real question, with no hedging. And she found that she was so frightened that she could hardly get the words out.

'Steve?' It wasn't much more than a croak.

He didn't meet her eyes, but she could see that he was afraid as well. 'I just—did it.'

'But you had to plan it out. You must have fetched the paraffin from the cellar and got it across here without letting anyone see, and—' Hannah felt herself beginning to bluster and get exasperated. That was safe enough. Stephen would never say a word if she carried on like that. Those were probably the things that were already running round and round his head. The things she should carry on saying, if she didn't really want to *know*.

Only Nick was watching her. She could feel it, even though she couldn't see him. And he had dared her. She took a deep breath and asked the real question. The one she had been afraid to ask.

'Was it me? Did I start you off, by forcing you to go and look for a weight?'

Stephen was amazed. He lifted his head and stared at her, wide-eyed. 'You? No, it was—' He tried for the words, failed and waved his hand at the lumpy little bundle lying on the stage in front of the guillotine.

Hannah walked over and picked it up. A grubby string bag, cobbled together with a bit of that frayed green string Doug always used. It was filled with clumsy, badly-finished carvings, done in wood that was too soft.

'Well, I know who made these,' she carried them across to Stephen, 'but I've never seen them before.'

He shied away from the bag. 'He gave them to me just after—' His eyes went blank for a second and he swallowed. 'Doug gave them to me.'

It got crazier and crazier. Hannah shook the bag under his nose. 'But he's given you lots of things. Birthday presents. Christmas presents. He's always giving us things. What's so special about these? And why did they make you want to burn the French Terror?'

'Doug,' Stephen said. He found her eyes, staring into them as if he could make her understand everything from that single word. '*Doug.*'

And suddenly, as though he had flipped a switch in her brain, she was there again, coming home from boarding school for the first time. Seven years old and running into the house with her arms held out. 'Daddy, Daddy, I'm back!' No one had warned her that everything had changed. No one told her anything, until Mother came in from putting the car away. *He's living on Uncle Ernest's side of the house, for the time being. It's better like this for a bit.* And her arms had dropped to her sides, slowly. She didn't remember ever holding them out to anyone like that again. Because he had left her. They had sent her away to boarding school and while she was there he had left her.

The memory was so sharp, so freshly painful that she closed her eyes as she forced the words out, accusingly. 'You always said that you didn't know what happened.'

'I—' Stephen fumbled for what he wanted to say. 'I don't *remember* what happened. But I think it must be there, in my head.'

'Well why don't you find out!' Hannah spat it at him, forgetting that Nick was even in the room, forgetting everything except how terrible it was to be careful and never say what you meant and never ask questions. How terrible it was not to *know*. 'If I had something like that in my head, messing me about, making me do crazy things, I'd *find out what it was*!'

Stephen went so white that she thought he was going to faint. He even swayed slightly on his feet. Then, suddenly, he reached out and grabbed the string bag from her. Without a word, he began to walk towards the door.

'What are you doing?' Hannah whirled round and screamed at him. 'Running away? As usual?'

He stopped with his hand on the door handle and shook his head. 'I'm going to find Mother. I'm going to make her tell me what happened.' And then he went, before she could even catch her breath.

Chapter 13

He walked through the gallery without even seeing it. The only thing he was aware of was the texture of the string between his hands. The bag was one way into the darkness, the only thing he could carry with him and hold under Mother's nose so that she couldn't ignore it. If he was brave enough.

But he had to know now, unless he wanted to spend the rest of his life hiding things and setting fire to things, without understanding why. His mind was quite made up, even though it took him twenty minutes to find Mother, twenty minutes in which he could hardly breathe for fear.

Whatever it was, he had to know.

He found her at last, in the linen closet, sorting through the piles of stiff white sheets with their embroidered monograms.

'Mother.'

'Back already?' She shook out a pillowcase and refolded it briskly. 'I thought you'd be a long time over there. You hurried off so fast you didn't even hear me call you.'

'Mother, I want you to tell me—'

'It's taken me rather a long time to do this all by myself.' She pulled a sheet off the pile and spread it out, examining the creases to see if there was any sign of wear. 'Have you got a moment to help me now?'

Automatically, Stephen put down the string bag and took the end of the sheet to help her refold it. And she caught sight of the string bag. He saw her notice it, hesitate for a second and then look away.

'Where's Hannah, then?' she said quickly.

There was only one way to get her to talk about what he

wanted, and that was to ignore everything she said. Stephen put the edges of the sheet together. 'Please will you tell me about that string bag?'

He saw the directness of the question shock her, catching her off guard, just for a second. Then she said, 'String bag?'

Stephen dropped the end of the sheet on the ground and picked up the bag. 'This string bag.'

'Really, Stephen, I don't know what you think you're doing! Now I shall have to wash this sheet. It's all dusty.' She turned away from him, bundling it together and pushing it into the linen bag. 'If you're too busy to concentrate properly, I can do this better without you.'

'I want to know about this string bag.' He stood there stubbornly, holding it out.

Mrs Roscoe did not even look at it. 'You can't expect me to remember every piece of rubbish that gets put away in the attics.'

For a second, Stephen watched as she took down another sheet, shook it and examined it. Then, very quietly, he said, 'I never told you that this came from an attic. You do remember it, you see.'

'Of course it came from an attic. That's where I put all the old, useless things.' But she was confused by her mistake and this time she did look at the bag, as though she had not noticed it before. 'Oh, *that* old thing,' she said carelessly, 'well, you can see what it is. Just some wooden animals that—someone—made for you when you were small. They're full of splinters. Not suitable at all. And anyway, you're much too old for that sort of thing now. I should throw them away.'

Stephen took out one of the swans and stroked its broken neck. 'It wasn't *someone* who made them for me, was it? It was Doug. He made them specially, because I liked the Noah's Ark automaton so much.' He shut his eyes, because he couldn't say the next bit while he was looking at her. 'He made them so that I'd know he still loved me, even though you forced him to go and live on the other side.'

'I didn't force him,' Mrs Roscoe said quickly.

'So what happened? Why did he go? Why don't we all live together?'

'We *do* live together.' She turned away from him and began to fold the sheet, briskly. 'It's just more—convenient for him to live on the other side, because of looking after Uncle Ernest.'

'Why don't we all live over there, then?'

It was very hard to get the words out. They never asked questions like that, and they never ever asked *Mother* questions like that. Stephen found that he had clenched his fists hard round the string of the bag. But he had to know. He had to force her to tell him.

'Please,' he said.

Mrs Roscoe tweaked the top of the sheet straight and put it on top of the pile. 'It's just better this way, that's all.'

He felt as though he was pushing against a bulldozer. She seemed so strong that it took every ounce of willpower he had to go on and on asking instead of just nodding and letting it pass.

'But what made it be better? It was all right when we came here, wasn't it? We all came together and lived over here. And then it happened suddenly, out of the blue, while Hannah was away at school. Why?'

No answer. Just her back turned to him, very still.

He took a deep breath. 'It's got something to do with this string bag, hasn't it? And the French Terror?'

No answer. She was taking down another sheet.

'Do you know what I've just done?' He said it deliberately. Cruelly. 'I've just poured paraffin all over the French Terror. It would be burning now, if Hannah and Nick hadn't come in and stopped me. *And I don't know why I did it.*'

That made her turn round all right. She stared at him with her eyes huge and horrified and her mouth opening and shutting, unable to speak. And suddenly Stephen understood, for the first time, why she would never let anyone speak to her about things she didn't want to hear. It wasn't because she was strong. It was because she was afraid.

That was the worst moment of all. If he had had any choice, he would have pretended not to notice anything, would have gone away quickly, and never talked about it again. But he had no choice.

'You see, you have to tell me what happened,' he said gently.

From somewhere she found a voice to speak to him with. Not her own level, controlled voice, but a feeble, breathless croak. 'But you *know* what happened, Stephen.'

He stared at her. 'No I don't. You've never told me.'

'I didn't need to tell you.' She closed her eyes, swallowed as if her throat were dry. 'You were there.'

Darkness. Something moving and—

His mind cut out. Refused to go on, however hard he pushed it. He shook his head. 'I may have been there, but I can't remember what happened. I was only four, wasn't I?'

'But you can't have forgotten—'

'Yes?' he said eagerly, waiting for her to go on.

She seemed to gather herself together. 'I'm not sure this is the kind of thing we ought to meddle with,' she said in a voice more like her own. 'If you have forgotten, that could be your mind protecting itself. Shall we let it be?'

That would have been a nice, comfortable way out for both of them, if he really had forgotten. But it wasn't so simple.

'What shall I do then?' he said relentlessly. 'Just go on setting fire to things?'

No way out, Mother. You have to tell me, however hard it is. And it was hard for her, no doubt about that. He could see her struggling not to cry. But she was trying to tell him and one more tiny push would do it. He just needed an extra lever . . . The words came automatically into his mouth.

'I shall go mad if I don't get this sorted out. *Please* don't back away from me when I need you.'

Her hand shot out sharply and gripped his wrist hard, as though he had said more than he knew. 'We'll go across,' she said. 'Perhaps—perhaps if I show you, you'll remember what—'

And then they were walking towards the stairs, and she

was still holding fast to his wrist, as though she might lose him for ever if she let go.

When Stephen walked out of the billiard room. Hannah was so surprised that she went on staring after him, even when he had disappeared.

'That's a pretty brave thing to do,' Nick said softly. 'Isn't it? *He's* stepped out of the pattern.'

O.K., so I'm the villain now and Steve's the hero. Hannah shrugged. 'Not much point to it though, is there? He'll never get Mother to tell him anything she doesn't want to. We still won't know what happened.'

She had spoken harshly because she was so tired of the whole thing, so furious with everyone in the family. And now Nick would think that she was hateful and horrible and he would probably go straight off to the library and bury himself in his beloved Samuel Roscoe's papers again, so that he could forget all about the nasty modern Roscoes.

But he didn't go. He looked at her curiously.

'If you're really so keen to know about what happened, why don't you find out for yourself? It's not like you to rely on someone else.'

'What?' She blinked at him.

'Nothing stopping you. Stephen's gone to ask your mother, but I would have thought your father was more likely to tell you.'

'Ask *Doug*?'

'Why not?'

Because he always wants to give us things and help us and be necessary to us. So we never ask him for anything. She hadn't known until Nick asked the question, but now she realized. Ask Doug for a cup of tea and he would make you a four course meal. Ask him to do up a screw and he would try to finish the job. There was no way of explaining all that to Nick.

'I—I just can't.'

He looked at her. 'Afraid?'

'Of course not!'

134

But she was afraid. Afraid of being smothered. And a bit afraid, as well, of what she might find out. But part of her mind wanted Nick to go on nagging at her and taunting her, to make her climb the stairs and knock on Uncle Ernest's door. She waited for him to ask why she didn't go then, and what was the matter with her, and didn't she really want to know.

Instead, he turned away, as though he felt he had said too much already. Embarrassed. 'I think I'd better get back to work now. Those papers—'

'Nick.' She interrupted quickly, before he could leave. 'If I go now—if I go up and ask—will you come with me?'

He looked surprised. 'I can't really do that, can I? I mean, it's private to your family.'

'But you saw Stephen with the paraffin just as much as I did. And—' Hannah hunted for another reason. 'And anyway, there's Uncle Ernest.'

Nick hesitated.

'Oh come on.' Now she had the idea of going, she couldn't bear to pass it up, but she wasn't sure she could do it without moral support. She tried unfair tactics. 'You were the one who started all this, after all. If you hadn't encouraged us to open the Collection, we'd never even have found the French Terror.'

Nick pulled a face, but he nodded. 'I suppose they ought to know about Stephen, anyway. We'll tell them that and see what happens.'

But he was obviously not very happy about coming. He didn't say anything while they were climbing the stairs, and he stood back and waited for Hannah to knock on the sitting room door.

'Come in.'

Not Doug's voice. Uncle Ernest himself, loud and clear. *Just my luck*, Hannah thought grimly. On the one day she wanted him to be totally senile, he was having one of his good days. Oh well, better get it over with. She pushed the door open.

Uncle Ernest was sitting in his wheelchair, facing her, looking amused. In front of him was Doug, sitting on a very low stool. He had Uncle Ernest's bare foot in his lap and a nail file in one hand. It was a pallid, yellowish foot with lumpy callouses and long thick nails that curved like horns.

Doug rose slightly, as though he meant to get up, but Uncle Ernest's hand was on his shoulder instantly, squashing him down. And Uncle Ernest's smile widened, a very little bit. It obviously pleased him to be discovered like that, with Doug crouching like a slave over his revolting foot.

Disgusting old man, thought Hannah. She smiled politely, and looked at Doug. 'Do you think we could have a word with you?'

'Yes, of course you can.' Doug made to get up again, and again Uncle Ernest squashed him down.

'You're cutting my toe-nails,' he said imperiously.

'Well, I—' Doug looked apologetically at Hannah. 'If you wait outside for a moment or two . . .'

'Then you're going to read to me,' Uncle Ernest said loudly.

'Of course, of course.' There was something cringe-making about the quick, soothing way Doug said it. Hannah shuddered inside. He was trying to please every-one. 'I'll just pop out and have a few words with Hannah before I start reading.'

'No you won't. If she's got anything to say, she can say it here.' Uncle Ernest glared at Hannah.

She wouldn't allow herself the luxury of glaring back. Instead, she gave him a sugary-sweet smile and spoke as stiffly as she could. 'I'd just like a moment or two alone. I've got something very important to say. To my father.'

Out of the corner of her eye, she saw Doug's surprised, pleased smile when she said it. Until the words were out of her mouth, she hadn't realized quite how unusual they were. *My father.* But before she had time to wonder why she had used them, Uncle Ernest was leaning forward to peer at her, as though he had heard more than she had spoken.

'So what do you want to say?' He fired the words at her. 'It's not something about the French Terror, is it? Hey? Have you run it?'

It was like having her mind read. Uncomfortable.

136

Terrifying. And Hannah could see that Doug was unpleasantly surprised as well, from the sharp way he glanced at Uncle Ernest and then at her. She looked sideways at Nick, for support.

'Hey?' Uncle Ernest said again. 'Have you run the French Terror?'

'We haven't run it yet,' said Nick. 'We're having a few problems finding a weight. But in the meantime, something—something rather upsetting has happened.'

He stopped, waiting for Hannah to explain, but before she could say anything, Doug was on his feet.

'I told you, Hannah, I told you the French Terror was dangerous and you ought to leave it alone. What have you been doing?'

He's angry, Hannah thought wonderingly. She didn't remember ever seeing him lose his temper before. There was something a bit comic about it. His voice got shriller, his face went red and the strand of hair he combed across his bald patch came loose and flapped about. But he suddenly seemed much more real than he had when he was sitting on a stool being careful not to offend Uncle Ernest.

'I haven't done any harm.' She was surprised to hear how defensive she sounded.

'Sit down, Doug,' Uncle Ernest said peevishly. 'None of your business. *I* asked them to mend the French Terror.'

'It's all in a good cause,' said Nick. Nice of him to join in, really, when he was obviously wishing he was safe in the library. Hannah gave him a quick smile. 'We're getting the Collection ready to open to the public, to raise some money for helping to repair the house.'

'You're—?' Doug looked startled. He glanced round at Uncle Ernest and gave him a long stare. Then he sat down on the stool again. 'All right. Tell us what happened.'

'It's—it's Stephen.' Hannah twisted her hands together behind her back. 'Nick and I just came in and found him—well, he was trying to set fire to the French Terror. And he didn't know why.'

Doug groaned softly and buried his face in his hands. 'Is he all right?'

'I think so,' Hannah said, hoping it was true. 'He's gone to see if Mother will explain to him why he—I mean—' It was ridiculously difficult to get the words out, but she was determined to do what she had come to do. Clenching her fists, she blurted out a question. 'What on earth is going on?'

Doug lifted his head and looked straight at her. 'You don't know what happened, that first term you were at boarding school? Alison's never told you?'

You must be joking. When would she ever tell us about anything difficult or painful? Somehow Hannah managed not to say it, but Doug understood anyway. He smiled ruefully.

'No. No, of course not. Well—' He was having a bit of trouble talking as well. He stared hard at the toes of his shoes and began to speak rather fast. 'When we first came here, I thought the way you do. Idiotic to let the place decay. Simple to make money out of tourists. And I decided to open the collection of automatons to the public.'

Hannah gasped.

'The handbills?' Nick said eagerly. 'You had the hand-bills printed?'

'Handbills printed, drive cleared, all ready to go. And the French Terror—'

'The French Terror!' Uncle Ernest shouted the words suddenly, drowning out Doug's voice. 'We should see it, not talk about it. Hannah can run it for us.'

'*Run* it?' said Doug.

Uncle Ernest gave him an extraordinarily spiteful smile. 'She can take the weight from the kitchen. *My* weight.' The smile sharpened. 'The weight Alison wouldn't give you.'

'But he hasn't told me—' Hannah didn't like being ordered around. Why couldn't Doug explain things to her before they went downstairs? What difference could it make?

Uncle Ernest obviously thought there was a difference. He glared at her. 'Get the weight, girl. Do as you're told.'

She held out for a second more, with them all looking at her, waiting to see what she would do. And then the irony of it hit her. She had spent hours and hours thinking about the

French Terror, trying to understand it, and here she was turning down a chance to see it run. She must be mad. Why not run the French Terror now? And if she did—

Something told her that all these things were tangled together. Doug and Mother and the house and the French Terror and Stephen with the paraffin. Grasp hold of one thread and it would take you to the centre in the end, as long as you kept hold of it. If you dared.

Turning her back on them all, she went, not bothering to say anything, leaving all the doors open behind her and closing her mind to what would happen next. She ran out of the room, up the stairs and across the gallery. To fetch the weights.

Chapter 14

It was like a dream, walking through the gallery with his mother. Neither of them spoke. There was no sound except the pad of their shoes on the wooden floor and the interminable roaring of the water, down the waterfall and underneath the house.

And, as if it were a dream, there were no barriers to slow them down. The door at the end of the gallery, which was always shut, swung open now and Mrs Roscoe swept Stephen through without pausing to knock or call. Straight along the corridor they went, and down the stairs.

They had reached the bottom before they heard the voices. Three of them, coming from the billiard room. Stephen hesitated for a second, with his foot on the last stair, working out who was in there. Doug. Nick. And— Uncle Ernest? It seemed incredible. He could never remember Uncle Ernest leaving his little circle of sitting room, bathroom and bedroom on the floor above. But this was a dream, and in dreams anything can happen.

Anything. Mother could even walk into the billiard room where the others were and speak to them.

'Good afternoon, Mr Honeyball. Hallo, Ernest. Hallo, Doug.'

Her face was very pale and her hand, gripping Stephen's wrist, clenched tighter, but no one could have guessed from her voice that anything unusual had happened.

Doug was the opposite, of course. He flushed bright red, took a step forward and then stopped. 'Alison—'

And then neither of them could speak. Years of silence, of avoiding each other had bound their tongues, so that they met in a place where there were no words. Ridiculous to be polite, impossible to say what they really felt. Stephen shrivelled inside, wishing that his mother would let go of his hand, so that he could escape.

Uncle Ernest gave a loud, hoarse chuckle and smacked his hand down hard on the upholstered leather bench where he sat. 'Only Hannah to come. Switch off the lights, Mr Honeyball, and light the candles.'

Nick had been staring at the painted ceiling, trying to pretend he wasn't there. Now he looked round, confused. 'I'm sorry?'

'Candles!' Uncle Ernest banged one end of his walking frame on the floor. 'That's how it was. That's how my grandfather did it when he showed me the French Terror.'

Candlelight. Shadows dancing on the walls and over the giant faces in the ceiling. And in the shadows, moving . . . Stephen closed his eyes.

But Nick was suddenly smiling, as if something had made sense to him. '*You!* You were the little boy in the sailor suit, in that photograph!'

And Uncle Ernest was nodding and rocking backwards and forwards on his seat. 'Candles. He made them light the candles because that's how it should be. Even though I was afraid of the dark. Afraid of the dark and afraid of him, because he was so old. *I'll show you something you'll remember all your life, boy.* That's what he said.'

'Then we must have the candles, if that's how he did it.' Nick began to hurry round the room, lighting the tall white candles that stood on either side of the French Terror.

'Alison.' Doug stepped closer to them and Stephen could feel his mother trying not to shrink away. 'I don't think this is a good idea.'

Mrs Roscoe lifted her chin. 'Stephen wants to remember what happened here when he was four.'

'*No,*' Doug said. 'It's crazy.'

He made her meet his eyes and for a moment they were staring at each other, both very determined and very still. But Stephen felt his mother's fingers tighten round his wrist.

'It will be all right,' she said. Her voice was cold and she looked immovable. But Stephen could see, now, how vulnerable she was.

Doug saw it, too. His challenging stare wavered, dropped. As if he had lost the right to try and persuade her to do what he wanted. He stepped back, leaving her free to move away from him.

Mrs Roscoe walked forward, still dragging Stephen after her, and laid a hand on the stage of the French Terror. For a second she stood quite still, running her fingertips over the polished wood and looking up at the looming framework of the guillotine. Then she glanced at him. 'You really don't remember?'

He shook his head.

She was just about to turn away when she caught sight of something on the far side of the stage, on the ground. Something that made her draw in her breath with a noise loud enough for Stephen to hear. He leaned forward to peer past her, so that he could see what it was.

Tins. Just a heap of different tins, with a condensed milk tin on top. For an instant he wondered whether they were Hannah's, whether she was in the habit of eating in here on her own. Then he saw how old and dirty the tins were, and there didn't seem to be any reason for the way his mother had reacted.

'Here's Hannah!' Uncle Ernest said. 'Put out the lights, Mr Honeyball.'

Hannah came running into the room with the big iron weight from the kitchen scales in one hand and a long brass cylinder in the other, just as Nick flicked the light switch. The sudden darkness caught her by surprise and she stopped halfway to the French Terror, staring at them all.

The heavy velvet curtains blocked out all the daylight and the candle flames jumped and guttered, sending long shadows in all directions across the room. Huge black humps squatted on the windowseat beside Uncle Ernest. Taller, thinner shadows rayed out from Stephen's feet towards his mother and Doug. From them to him. And between the two of them. And long and slanting, stretching from the centre of the room to the door that connected with the collection room, the shadow of the French Terror sprawled over the floor.

Inside Stephen's head, something moved, as though a door had opened a crack, just wide enough to let out the sound of a voice. *I have been here before, like this.* And he was afraid.

'What's going on?' Hannah said, sounding annoyed. 'Why the candles?'

Her eyes flicked round the room and Stephen saw her take in who was there. Not only Doug and Nick and Uncle Ernest. Mother, too. She stood very still, as though she was waiting for something.

'Come on, girl, come on,' Uncle Ernest said irritably. 'Have you got the weights?'

Hannah held them up, one in each hand.

'Go on, then. Fix them up.'

She hesitated for a second, glancing at Stephen as though he could tell her what was happening. But he felt frozen, unable to say anything to anyone. After a second or two, she shrugged, walked across to the French Terror and vaulted up on to the stage.

'I don't *know* it's going to work,' she said to the room at large. 'I think I've understood it, and I think the missing weight was the only problem, but I can't be sure. So don't be too disappointed if there's just a nasty noise, will you?'

Reaching a hand into the back of the right hand guillotine pillar, she caught hold of the cord that dangled inside. Stephen could see her feel for the end, because he could see through the hole in the front of the pillar. But before she could tie on the weight, a voice interrupted her.

'No,' said Mrs Roscoe.

She turned suddenly and pulled the string bag out of Stephen's hand. With a quick impatient gesture, she tipped the wooden animals out of it, letting them clatter on to the floor. Then she held the bag out to Hannah.

'Not the weight from the kitchen,' she said. 'Use the tins.'

It took Hannah a second or two to realize what she meant.

Tins? And the bag? Then Doug put his face in his hands and groaned, and she got it. *The weight Alison wouldn't give you. That* was why the tins had been in the machinery. Mother had refused the kitchen weight last time, as well, when Doug had wanted it. So Doug had invented a substitute. A typical piece of hopeful bodging.

Still, there was no reason that she could see why it shouldn't work, assuming that the tins were the right weight. She hopped off the stage, took the bag from Mother and walked over to the neat little pyramid she had made on the far side of the room.

As she bent down to load the tins into the bag, she could feel everyone else in the room watching her. Could feel them almost holding their breath. As she wriggled the baked bean tins round the peas, and settled the spaghetti hoops on top, she had an eerie feeling that she was acting out what Doug had done all those years ago. The tins had to sit just right, or they wouldn't fit into the bag. Beans and peas on the bottom, peaches and spaghetti hoops next, condensed milk—still sticky—on the very top. Not just any old bodge-up. The same bodge-up as before, repeating itself.

Don't be stupid. You're Hannah, not Doug. Things don't repeat themselves.

She climbed up on to the stage, reached for one of the loose ends of cord and tied the bag inside the left hand pillar. Everyone else waited, not really looking at her now, but just willing her to finish.

It was only when she picked up the brass cylinder that she realized what she had done. She had reversed the weights, so that the bag was hanging where the cylinder had been before. Quickly she glanced down into the room. No one seemed to have noticed. Shouldn't make any difference, anyway. The weights were supposed to be equal. Quickly she tied the cylinder inside the right hand column and jumped off the stage.

'O.K. then. Shall I start it?'

The clump of black shadows on the windowseat stirred as Uncle Ernest nodded. Mrs Roscoe caught hold of Stephen again and pulled him back until he was standing in the doorway that led through to the Collection room.

'Come over here, Hannah,' she said sharply. 'As soon as you've turned it on. And you, Mr Honeyball. And Doug.'

Even Doug? Very cosy, Hannah thought sourly as she moved round to the back of the French Terror. No need to wind it. All she had to do was flick the lever.

She did it with a flourish. 'Here you are then, everybody. The marvellous, the amazing, the unique—French Terror!'

Then she skipped down the room and stood beside the others, watching. For a moment there was nothing. Only a few creaks from behind the doors at the back of the stage. Then the doors opened smoothly and a figure walked out on to the stage, head bowed, feet moving in small, regular steps.

Hannah had examined that figure carefully. She knew all about the machinery under the flowing skirts, about the levers that worked the legs and the expanding rod that kept it steady. But even she nearly caught her breath as the candlelight flickered over the elegant, poised hands, the small, slippered feet and the lowered head with its perfect features. If she hadn't known, she might almost have thought, might almost have believed . . .

The figure advanced until it was framed by the pillars of the guillotine and the dangerous diagonal blade hanging overhead. Slowly it looked up until it was staring straight at the little group of watchers. For a second it was still. Then, very gently, one hand moved, the lips parted slightly and the eyelids blinked.

You devil, Hannah said in her mind, thinking of the unknown maker. *You meticulous, clever devil.*

Even while she was thinking it, the figure bent forward to rest its neck on the guillotine bar. The pause was exactly, beautifully timed. Hannah was watching for the little extra dip that would work the switch and bring the guillotine blade crashing down, but even she hardly noticed it. One moment the figure of a beautiful woman was bent over underneath it, and the next there was a rattle and a thud. The head crashed down, disconnected from the neck, into the basket in front of the guillotine. Through the hole in the right hand pillar, Hannah saw the brass cylinder rise to waist height, balancing the guillotine blade.

Then the body collapsed on to its front and slid away backwards through the doors, as if it were being dragged by the feet. At the same moment, simply and unobtrusively, the bottom of the basket slid open and the severed head disappeared on to the moving belt beneath.

'Extraordinary,' Nick said. 'I never thought—'

'Sssh!' Mrs Roscoe's voice was harsh. 'Wait!'

The doors closed. Behind them, the machinery creaked for a second or two before they opened again. This time it was the figure of the man who appeared.

The shock of the realism had gone now, after the first time, and Hannah could look at the whole thing more mechanically. She ticked off the movements in her head, trying to work out how each one was produced. One step forward—two—three—four. Raise head. Pause. Hand and lips and eyelids move. Bend forward and—now!

Crash! The blade fell, the body slid away and the head vanished, just as before. This time, Hannah noticed the weights fall again and the guillotine blade rise as the figure moved backwards to the doors.

All ready for the next victim. Round and round in a perfect, pre-ordained circle. Death and death and death.

And it was the boy. As he appeared, something changed in the atmosphere of the room. Mrs Roscoe tensed, Uncle Ernest sat up straighter on the windowseat and Doug half-turned away.

'What—?' Hannah began.

Stephen flicked his hand against her arm. 'Ssh!' Glancing sideways at him, Hannah saw that he was staring at the stage almost without blinking, his eyes reflecting the pattern of shadows and moving flames around it.

One step—two—three—four. Hannah swallowed as the boy moved to the guillotine. He was the most real of all, as though his face had been sculpted like an actual face. She was glad she knew about the cogs and the cams and the rods that made him work, because otherwise it would have been impossible not to think that living boys had once walked like that, towards death. Perhaps a boy with that very face . . .

It was an obscene toy. It made a game of something that should never be thought of except with rage and shame and fear. Hannah closed her eyes so that she would not see the death again, but her ears picked up the faint whirr of the machinery, the rattle of the guillotine blade, the thud of the severed head and told her, relentlessly, what was happening.

Until, suddenly, they registered a noise that was wrong. A faint grating, grinding sound. Hannah opened her eyes quickly and saw the guillotine blade rising awkwardly, pulled higher on the right hand side than on the left. What on earth—?

Then she saw what had happened. Inexplicably, the boy's arm had hooked round the cord from the right hand pillar and the headless body, as it moved back towards the doors, was dragging the brass cylinder with it.

Stupid to let it get tangled in the works. Stupid to let the thing get broken now that it was mended at last. With a quick, impatient sigh, Hannah ran forward to the stage.

Chapter 15

He didn't know. He didn't remember until the very last second. The door in his mind was still almost closed and he felt as though it imprisoned him in a tiny, airless room that cramped smaller and smaller round him as the figures of the French Terror moved to their executions.

The woman. Then the man. And then—as the boy appeared, Stephen found that he could hardly breathe, that his whole body was focussed on the stage, drawn towards it by the fascination of terror. When Hannah spoke to him, he hissed 'Ssh!' at her, without even hearing what it was that she had said. Every muscle in his body was tense and his chest was tight. Round his wrist, fierce and painful, were his mother's fingers, but the pain seemed to have nothing to do with what was going on inside him. It was just another thing in the room.

And he still didn't know, didn't remember. There was nothing in his head except a blind, black fear.

The guillotine fell, the boy's head dropped. Now! said his brain, *Now!* Like a nightmare, forgotten until that instant, the guillotine blade rose crooked, higher on the right side than on the left. Stephen felt his mother pull him backwards, automatically shrinking away.

First she wouldn't give up the weight, and then she jumped backwards instead of forwards. She'll be guilty for ever. Backwards instead of forwards, backwards instead of forwards . . .

In the same fraction of a second, Hannah gave a quick sigh of impatience, darting forward down the room, and the door flew open in Stephen's mind, letting in horror like a searing blaze of light. He *knew*. He knew what had happened, what would happen again. No time to speak or shout or warn. All he could do was move.

He flung himself down the room after Hannah, grabbed at her legs and brought her crashing to the ground at the very foot of the stage, so that she caught her cheek on the corner.

Even before they fell, he saw the boy's arm move again, letting go of the cord, letting the weight swing back towards them. A murderous pendulum. It swept through the hole in front of the pillar and whistled over their heads, so close that Stephen felt the wind of its passing.

And *pain*.

It didn't touch them, it was probably two or three inches from his ear, but all along the right hand side of his head he felt a blow as if he had been scalped, as if he had been flayed with cudgels, the skin scraped off and the flesh bruised and torn.

Yes, *yes*. That's how it was. And he could see, not the bare polished boards that were really in front of his eyes, but the orange pattern of the bag as it swung away from him, the string criss-crossing over the letters he was too young to read, the letters that said *Baked beans*.

And then there had been the shouting. Mother had—

In the instant that he thought it, it began again, as though by thinking he had made it happen. As though this raging, screaming mother was a monster he had hidden in his brain all these years. And now he had let her out, and she was yelling and clawing with her nails and frothing with spit at the corners of her mouth. Not a memory, but *real*.

She threw herself at Doug, battering his face with her hands. 'You let her run! You let Hannah run, and it nearly happened again! *Again!* They could both have been killed this time! Both their heads—smashed!'

Smashed! Smashed! She had yelled it like that before, grotesquely, demented. He had been lying on the floor, dazed, with the side of his head bleeding, and somehow it was all his fault and the room was full of anger, exploding between Mother and Doug, breaking things apart, breaking them up.

'Smashed! Smashed!' she had yelled, out of control,

while Stephen clenched his fists and gritted his teeth, waiting for Doug to catch hold of her and stop the yelling and the anger and the fear.

But he hadn't. He had stood still, white-faced, letting her hammer him, letting her scratch his cheeks and scream abuse at him, as if he couldn't defend himself. And then, just as Stephen was about to scream himself, because he couldn't bear it any more, Doug had—Doug had—

That was it, Stephen pressed his knuckles hard against his forehead. That was the worst thing of all, the thing his mind had been hiding from him all these years.

Doug had crumpled to the ground, kneeling forward with his head huddled into his arms, and he had begun to cry. Horrible, ugly sobs that shook him almost to pieces. It was like the floor giving way or the sky cracking across the middle. Stephen wanted to black his mind out, faint, lose his memory—anything to shut out that picture of Doug collapsed on the floor, with Mother shrieking at him.

But there was no escape, because now, here—in the real world—Mrs Roscoe was screaming again. The words were deformed and twisted, so that it was hard to make them out. Sentences and phrases leapt out at Stephen, but he didn't know if they came from his memory or her mouth.

' . . . pathetic, incompetent idiot . . . can't do anything without bungling it . . .not fit to have children . . .'

It was all happening exactly the same, all over again. And next—and next Doug would—

I can't watch it. Stephen scrambled to his feet, put his head down and ran out of the room, pushing Nick aside and ignoring Hannah's voice as she called after him. He had to get away, into the fresh, clean, empty air, where there were no people, no shouts, no anger.

He threw himself along the lobby and out of the door and, without consciously making a decision, began to run up the narrow, steep path to the broken bridge, panting and stumbling on the uneven surface.

It was raining. Not hard. Just a faint, fine drizzle that seeped down through the trees and prickled his skin. He ran with his head lowered, not seeing anything except the patch of ground beneath his feet, not noticing how the rain plastered his hair against his head and soaked through the shoulders of his tee-shirt. On and on, not looking, not thinking, almost blind.

And then, suddenly, before he was ready, he was on the bridge, running at top speed towards the gap in the middle. There was no time to stop, because his feet were slippery on the wet stones. As he reached the end, he saw the water foam, way below, and then, instinctively, he launched himself forwards, without working out if it was safe, without caring what would happen to him.

His feet landed on more wet, slippery stones and slid away from him. Desperately he grabbed at one of the rowan trees that was rooted in the stonework, wrenching it hard before he found his footing and hauled himself on to the other side of the bridge. Then, panting and exhausted, he sank on to the stones, huddling behind the parapet, hidden from any eyes that might look up from the house. The rowan tree dripped water on to his face and dark, wet bushes brushed his shoulder, but he was blind to what was around him.

He remembered everything now. Nine years ago. The pictures formed in his mind, one by one, not linked together with explanation and understanding, but bright and separate and devastating. A four year old's pictures.

It had been such a wonderful, special day. He had picked that up, even though he didn't understand why. Something good was going to happen, something connected with the roomful of moving toys, and Doug had brought him down there, with Mother, to show off what he had done.

Magic toys. Animals that moved. Soldiers that really marched, birds that sang. And the Noah's Ark, with the animals going in two by two, nodding their heads and flapping their wings, wriggling and trotting and creeping. Oh yes, he remembered that all right. He had held out his hands, imagining the games he could make with them, not understanding that they were fixed to a moving wheel.

'The animals! Daddy, please can I have the animals to play with?'

And everyone had laughed, but gently so that he knew he hadn't done anything wrong. Mother kissed him and Doug ruffled his hair.

And then.

'Aren't you going to show him the French Terror?'

Uncle Ernest's voice. He was sure it was Uncle Ernest who had said that. And Mother hadn't liked it. She hadn't said anything—she wouldn't do that—but she had given Doug one of those looks that made Stephen tighten all his muscles until his stomach hurt.

'It's all right, Alison.' Doug had said that, and got her smiling again. *'I haven't taken the weight from the kitchen. I've got something else that I think will work. We could try it now.'*

The bag with the tins. He had even shown it off to them before he hung it inside the pillar, because he was so proud of his ingenuity. Only Stephen hadn't understood why it was clever, and Mother had stopped smiling again.

That made sense. She hated bodging. Stephen could guess, now, that Doug had actually preferred to put a heap of tins into a bag, because he liked to improvise. But, to Mother, that would have been messy incompetence.

Then, all he knew was that the day was somehow less special, less happy. More like the ordinary days when Mother didn't speak much and Doug made jokes to try and cheer her up, jokes that she never laughed at.

And it had got dark. Dark and shadowy, because Uncle Ernest insisted on having the curtains pulled in the billiard room and the candles lit. So that when the first figure came through the doors at the back of the French Terror, Stephen had thought it was a real person, a woman in funny clothes, walking in a peculiar way. When there was a thud and her head fell off, he had screamed and clutched at his mother's hand, hiding his face in her skirt.

It's all right. Look. They're only dolls.

Who had said that? Doug? Uncle Ernest? Stephen couldn't be certain, but he knew he had lifted his head to look as the figure of the man came through the doors. And when that execution was finished, it had certainly been Uncle Ernest who spoke.

Go up closer and have a good look at the next one.

Closer.

He remembered walking down the room and standing right in front of the stage, looking up at the tall shape of the guillotine. And then everything had come together. The pain of the blow on his head, his mother's terrifying screams, and Doug—

Stephen's memory made it go on for ever, for hours, but he must have been wrong. Because the string bag had swung back like a pendulum after it hit him. Had crashed against one of the open doors at the back of the stage and split, spilling tins with. a clatter on to the wood. That couldn't have taken more than a second. And by the time the tins started to roll back through the open doors and into the machinery, he had been in Mother's arms, gripped too tightly, feeling her chest heave as she sobbed and struggled for breath. And Doug was on the ground with his face hidden.

He thought he'd killed me by bodging up the weight.

And Mother didn't want to remember about refusing the other weight. Or about flinching backwards when she should have run forwards to save me.

He could understand what had been going on now. But then it had all been incomprehensible, as if his world had gone crazy for no reason. Which made everything doubly frightening.

He had been in bed for days and days afterwards, and when he got up, things were different. Doug didn't live in their part of the house any more. He still came across sometimes—he'd come to bring the carved animals—but he was separated, sent away. Better not to ask why. Because the answers were there already, hidden somewhere down in the dark. Better not to disturb them.

Only now the door was open and they wouldn't go back.

Idiot!

Hannah felt like weeping with rage at her own brainlessness when she heard the weight swing back over her head. Fancy not asking herself what had ripped that hole in the paper front of the pillar! Fancy not *guessing* that it was the weight! But how on earth—?

Before she could even begin to think about it, all hell was let loose. Mother—*Mother*—started shouting and screaming as if they'd all been killed. As far as Hannah could see, the only injury around was the cut she'd got on her cheekbone when Stephen knocked her to the ground, and she could hardly gripe about that. He had probably saved her life. But Mother was yelling and carrying on and Doug was scarlet, with his fists clenched. No wonder Nick looked bewildered. The only calm one was Uncle Ernest on his windowseat.

And then Stephen stood up and bolted for the door.

'Hey, Steve!' Hannah yelled after him. 'You O.K.?'

No answer. He just ran out and across the lobby and a second later she heard his feet crunch on the gravel as he started up the slope towards the bridge.

Mother stopped screaming, as though she had run out of sound, and her face turned a dead, blank white. 'Stephen—?'

Doug shook his head at her, not unkindly, but almost as if he was pitying her. 'You wanted him to remember, Alison.'

'But I didn't think he would—'

There was a terrible, empty silence.

It was broken by a chuckle. A dry, bitter chuckle that went on and on. They all turned to look at Uncle Ernest and suddenly his face was split by a savage grin.

'Thought you knew all about Samuel Roscoe, didn't you?' He darted his head forward, growling out the words at Nick. 'You were all set to make a hero of him. *Him!*' His pointing finger stabbed fiercely at the French Terror. '*That* was what he did to me. Only six, I was, but he thought I needed toughening up.'

He's gone totally mad, Hannah thought. *Finally flipped.* It was Doug who had bodged up the bulky, awkward bag of

154

tins that had caught in the works and swung back. And it was Mother who had made him do it, by refusing the weight from the kitchen. So what had Samuel Roscoe got to do with anything?

Mother and Doug and Nick were all looking confused as well, but Uncle Ernest didn't seem to care. His smile turned venomous.

'Well, I'm toughened now. Tough enough to have the last word. To get my own back on him and his precious house that he cared so much about.'

'The house?' Nick muttered it, almost to himself, but Uncle Ernest heard.

'The house!' he repeated, triumphant. 'He loved it more than he loved my father, his own son. More than all of us. But it's mine now, and it's never going to have another slate on the roof, or another coat of paint. When I die, it will drop into the beck, and that will be the end of Samuel Roscoe. Destroyed by his own French Terror.'

He was rambling. He was raving and rocking backwards and forwards as he pointed past them all, at the empty stage with its broken guillotine. Inside the right hand pillar, through the hole in the paper, they could see the brass weight still swinging, as if it kept time with him. Backwards and forwards, backwards and forwards . . .

The *brass* weight.

They all saw it at the same time. Nick yelped as he realized and Mother clutched sharply at the door behind her. The brass weight was swinging gently inside the right hand pillar where Hannah had hung it by mistake. Where the bag of tins had been hung when Stephen was four. And this time it was the brass weight which had been caught and pulled back by the boy's arm.

And there was nothing makeshift about that. It was the original weight, with no awkward corners, no projections, hanging exactly as the maker had designed it to hang. Doing exactly what he intended it to do. Terrifying anyone who watched the French Terror for fun.

Whatever had been hanging inside the right hand pillar would have caught and swung in just the same way.

Hannah closed her eyes and felt the past alter. All those years. All those years of blame and guilt and separation sparked by a swinging bag of tins, when all the time—

'Samuel Roscoe set the pattern.' Nick sounded as if he were choking. 'And when it was set—'

He stared at Uncle Ernest, and Hannah wondered if he was seeing the small boy in the photograph. The boy in the sailor suit who had not really been toughened, but only terrified and changed. The boy who had had the French Terror buried deep in his mind, just as Stephen had, but who didn't want to destroy it. Only to make the pattern over again. And again.

Nick screwed his hand up and knocked the fists together, hard. 'It's all my fault, isn't it? If I hadn't come stirring things up—if I didn't have such a stupid, romanticized obsession with Samuel Roscoe—none of this would have happened.'

'You've only stirred up the truth,' Mrs Roscoe said, in a strange voice. But she didn't look at him, because she was staring at Doug. Not speaking. Just staring as if she couldn't fit him neatly into a corner of the pattern any more. And he was staring back, very white and very still.

Suddenly, fiercely, Hannah felt a surge of something strong and terrifying. It took her a second or two to understand that it was hope. *Go on, Mother. Tell him you're sorry. That we can all get together again now. Say it.*

But nobody spoke. Looking down at her own hands, Hannah saw that they were clenched tight, shaking. She was afraid too. Because, at least they'd survived the last nine years, in a funny, twisted way. They had stuck together in the same house, all one family even if it was a peculiar one. But it had been a precarious balancing trick. If they started messing about with it now, even to make things better, they would disturb that balance.

And suppose they failed?

Coward! Hannah snarled inside her head, not knowing which of the three of them she was raging at. She forced out the only words she dared to speak aloud.

'Don't you think it's time we went to look for Stephen?'

He heard them coming long before he saw them. Heard their feet slither on the steep, uneven path and their bodies brush past the bushes. But there was nowhere he could go. He cowered back against the tangle of undergrowth that blocked the way off the bridge on his side and closed his eyes tightly.

Three sets of feet? Four? He didn't really care who had come or what they wanted. It was too late for talking. He just wished they would go back and leave him on his own.

'Stephen?' said Mother's voice. And then, when she saw exactly where he was, '*Stephen!*'

He screwed his eyes tighter until stars swam behind the eyelids. *No. Go away. I can't take any more.*

'We want to talk to you, Stephen.'

That was Doug's voice. But it was brisker than he would have expected. And nearer. In spite of himself, Stephen opened his eyes.

There were four of them facing him across the stream. Hannah and Mother were standing close together on the bank and Nick was a little behind them, gazing down into the stream as if he was embarrassed to be there. But Doug was out in front, on the other half of the bridge, as though he had taken charge and led them all up there.

'That's right.' He nodded at Stephen and smiled. 'Now we can talk.'

Fiercely Stephen shook his head. There had been enough words. All the talking in the world wasn't going to alter the way things were. He felt as though he never wanted to do anything ever again, except stand here on the bridge, watching the clean, cold water of the waterfall roar down the rocks and into the pool. With a safe, empty gap between him and everyone else.

'*Yes,*' said Doug. 'We must—'

But as he was speaking, Nick interrupted suddenly, frowning.

'I don't like the look of that bridge.'

Stephen peered over the edge of the parapet. From the stonework under one of the rowan trees—the one he had grabbed to haul himself up—a trickle of mortar was running, dropping in a rain of dust and tiny lumps into the water below. Dropping down, with the water, on to the sharp rocks and into the deep pool.

'I should get back over here,' Doug said quietly.

But before Stephen could move, two lumps of stone, each as big as his fist, fell from the underside of the bridge and landed in the water with a double splash. And Mrs Roscoe shouted shrilly.

'Stephen! Jump! Jump *now*!'

Until that moment, he had been calm, watching the stonework crumble as if it had nothing to do with him. But the fear in her voice knocked the breath out of him and set his heart thumping. He gripped the bridge hard with both hands, keeping utterly still, hardly blinking. Because it seemed that if he moved a centimetre the bridge would break up completely and send him crashing down.

'Come on, now,' Doug said. 'Calm down.'

Another large stone splashed into the pool and Mrs Roscoe pressed her hands against her mouth with a small, sharp noise that would have been a scream if she had let it be. Stephen saw her whole body go tense with the effort of keeping silent.

Her terror paralysed him. Keep still. He must keep still, or else everything would come to pieces. The bridge would fall. Mother would shriek and go wild again, and Doug would fall to the ground and— It was sure to happen, the moment he moved, like an action replay. Over and over and over again, exactly the same as before. The only way he could control it, the only way he could keep the world together was by *not moving*.

He saw them all waving and shouting to him from the other side of the stream, but the words were tiny and faraway, swallowed up somewhere in the great empty space in between. Nothing reached him except the sight of mouths uselessly opening and shutting. Nothing made any sense except the two words in his head.

Keep still.

And then Doug stopped calling, as though he understood that it was no use. Stephen saw him turn and say something over his shoulder, and then he held out his hand to Mrs Roscoe.

For a second, Stephen thought she was going to ignore it. She looked down, at the crumbling, treacherous stonework and seemed to shrink back from the bridge. But then, slowly and steadily, not looking down, she began to walk forwards, towards Doug.

She came right up beside him, almost to the jagged, broken end of the arch, and then at last she did look down, not at the stones but at his hand, which he was still holding out.

She won't—she wouldn't ever—Stephen didn't understand what was happening, or why, but he had stopped noticing the sharp, rough parapet under his hands or the sound of the falling mortar. All he could see was the two hands—his mother's and Doug's—with a foot of empty space between them.

Very slowly, Mrs Roscoe's hand reached out to touch Doug's. One by one, her fingers closed round it, until the two of them were holding hands. Then they looked up at Stephen.

Not a magic, fairytale ending to all their troubles. Just Mother and Doug holding hands. But it meant that perhaps—. Maybe. If they all tried together.

And if Stephen jumped back across the stream.

He wanted it so much that it was unbearable, so much that he couldn't even let himself hope.

'I can't!' he yelled at them, across the water. 'I can't! You'll let me fall! It's impossible!'

He watched them look at each other and he saw that they didn't know what to say. But from behind them, shouted at the top of Nick's voice, came his answer.

'You can't say it's impossible until you've tried. *Every-*

thing difficult looks impossible. You live in an impossible house!'

Stephen looked down over the waterfall and saw the ridiculous, triumphant arch of Roscoe's Leap, spanning the stream. *You can't*, the world had said, but stubborn, cantankerous Samuel Roscoe had said *I can*, and changed the whole valley with the castle of his dreams.

Then he looked back at Mother and Doug, standing side by side and hand in hand. Just as impossible as Roscoe's Leap.

'Now,' said Doug.

And, with a great cry, Stephen leapt across the gap, into their arms.

A Tale of Three Houses

Most of my books start out like jigsaws. Two or three unconnected pieces come together, suddenly, in my head. They don't usually make a whole story—often, they're nothing like a story—but if they fit together in a certain way I get an unmistakable shiver down my back. That's when I know I can start to write the book.

It took three houses to give me the shiver that led to *Roscoe's Leap*.

The first was a strange, remote place in the Welsh hills, at Capel-y-ffin. It was built as a monastery in the nineteenth century and was occupied afterwards by a community of artists. We walked to see it once, when we were on holiday, and I never forgot its mysterious seclusion and the odd, unsettled atmosphere surrounding it.

I thought then that it would be good to write a book about the place, but there was no shiver to set me off. I brooded over the Welsh hills and thought about artistic communities, but I knew that there was nothing else I could do except wait for the next piece of the jigsaw to slide into place.

I didn't expect it to be another house, but it was. A very different one, though—Cragside, in Northumberland. Like the monastery at Capel-y-ffin, it was built in the nineteenth century, but not as an austere home for monks and artists. It was built for Sir William Armstrong, a very rich inventor and arms manufacturer. It is a rambling, romantic building, set on a steep slope, on a ledge blasted out of the rock. It doesn't bridge a stream, but it has a strong link with water because the lift and lots of other household machines were worked by water power, from specially made lakes above the house. These hydraulic machines were designed by Sir William Armstrong himself, who also had electric lights installed. Cragside was the first private house to be lit by electricity.

I was fascinated by it. As we drove away, the extraordinary house with its hundred rooms and its bizarre machinery, joined up, in my head, with the atmosphere of Capel-y-ffin. Without knowing anything about the characters or the plot, I knew that I was going to write a book.

But if I was going to write a book about Cragside/Capel-y-ffin, there were things I needed to find out about. I went to my local library (which is usually the best place to start) and hunted out books about hydraulics. I planned to fill the house in my book with strange and eccentric hydraulic machines and I needed to find out how they would work.

Quite often, when I start a story, I need to research subjects I don't know anything about. I'm quite used to reading dozens of books and going to special libraries to look up obscure details, and it doesn't daunt me at all. But when I started to read the books on hydraulics something dreadful happened.

I couldn't understand them.

For a week or two I battered my brains and wished I'd learnt more Maths and Physics at school, but at last I had to give in. I was never going to understand hydraulics. And if I couldn't understand how the hydraulic system worked in my imaginary house, then I couldn't believe in it. And if I couldn't believe in it—I couldn't write the book.

I was close to abandoning the whole idea when I remembered a third house built in the nineteenth century. Not a house for people, but a house for beautiful things. The Bowes Museum.

It stands near Barnard Castle, looking like a French château that has been picked up and put down in the English countryside, and it's full of furniture and clothes and china. But the most fascinating thing in it—the thing that slid into my jigsaw, in place of the hydraulics—is the Silver Swan.

The Silver Swan is a life-size clockwork automaton, but it's ridiculous to describe it like that. It is as beautiful as a piece of jewellery and far more wonderful. The huge silver swan swims on crystal waves that seem to flow past it, and from time to time it curves its neck down to dip its beak into the water. When it lifts its head, it's holding a fish that disappears into its mouth.

I remembered the Swan—and the Swan gave me the real,

162

unmistakable shiver. *That's what should be in my book!* I thought. So I began to read about eighteenth-century clockwork automata. And I discovered amazing things— like the Jaquet-Droz writer, which is a life-size model of a child, as realistic as a waxwork. The clockwork mechanism can be programmed by levers at the back, to make the child write any message of up to twenty-four letters. It dips its pen into the inkwell, looks from side to side, and actually writes the words on paper, in neat, elegant writing.

It was the Jaquet-Droz writer which led me to invent the French Terror, but I don't remember knowing much else about the book before I started writing it. I certainly didn't know what *happened*. I just told myself the story as I went along and then went back and tidied up the plot afterwards so that everything worked properly. I never worried that I wouldn't be able to finish it. I knew it could be written, because the three pieces of my jigsaw fitted so smoothly together.

The clockwork of the Bowes Museum.

The grandeur and machinery of Cragside.

And the eerie atmosphere of the Monastery at Capel-y-ffin.

Gillian Cross